Freakass Squirrels

by Patrick MacAdoo

Freakass Squirrels

ISBN - 978-0-990-9656-5-7

Printed in the United States

Chapter One

Snarls gurgled out of the maw of the monster. Its pelt spasmed. Individual follicles receded into swelling boils, which glowed sickly gray in the moonlight. The boils shrunk. A knobby spine crackled and strained against sweaty, acne-scared skin.

A squelch forced a flinch out of Pud. A reeking blast of body odor invaded Pud's nose and mouth, and seethed down his throat. Pud flailed away and fell to his hands and knees in the tall grass. Vomit hurtled up from the pit of his stomach and shot out of his mouth and nostrils. He felt like he was gonna die. The jet of his stomach's contents splatted against the ground.

Violent contractions cramped his empty guts. Tears blurred his vision. Stringers of drool hung from his lips and clung to grass stalks. He scrabbled away from his sudsy puke. He breathed a shuddery, "No."

Over ... *there*, a belt buckle clinked. Squint mumbled, "Sorry. You'd never believe me unless I showed you."

Squint ratcheted up his zipper and cinched his belt. Tears still blurred Pud's vision enough to obscure the scars speckling Squint's torso. Squint pulled his blue tee shirt over his head. With a deep sigh, Squint lowered himself into the grass. He pulled on his sallow tube socks, then his tattered sneakers.

Pud plopped onto his ass. He tried to spit out the stink. He blinked his eyes clear. Warmth, stoked by the eight or so Vartzes he'd already absorbed into his bloodstream, overcame his icy shock and fuzzed back into his brain. Squint sat in the grass on the other side of the clearing like nothing the fuck in the world just happened.

Squint returned Pud's stare. Pud hated to admit it, but at some point over the last year, Squint's misaligned teenaged features had matured into something near handsome. Squint narrowed his eyes and crinkled his forehead, scrunching his face into his familiar ugly squint. Somehow his hair even seemed thinner. He'd transformed into the runty six-grader whose family couldn't afford to get him glasses.

Pud raked his damp bangs away from his eyebrows. "Jesus Fucking Christ."

Squint dropped his gaze. Shadows darkened the creases of his face. He swiped his forearm across his mouth. He reached for the remnants of the case of beer. Four or five cans banged against one another as he dragged the cardboard carton toward his lap. Squint fished a can out of the carton. He fumbled with the flip top a couple of times. A carbonated hiss warned of a potential foam-over. Squint got the can to his mouth without losing a drop. He lowered the can and grimaced.

Pud's heartbeat throbbed hard enough to disturb his forehead. He flicked his sandpapery tongue over his dry lips. He raised his hand for a beer. Squint underhanded him one. Pud bobbled the catch, but managed to tip the can into a two-handed grab. He had more trouble working his index finger under the pop top. He rushed the open can to his mouth and drank too fast. The warm beer threatened to fizz right back up his throat. He flexed his stomach muscles and choked down the froth. He took another drink, wincing at the painful swallow. He zeroed in on Squint and said, "Nobody knows?"

Squint screwed up his features another notch. He shook his head. "Just my family. You know, the others."

"There's others?"

Squint took a long pull off his beer. He scanned the trees surrounding the little clearing in the woods. Pud imagined Squint, and maybe a few others, changing into bigbutt squirrels and jumping from treetop to treetop …

"Holy Shit!" Pud said. "You could climb up goddamned Big Rock and clean that bullshit off!" Those hateful words were seared into his brain. The green paint made them glow in the dark. When he was a little kid, every time they drove by on the way to the city, he'd asked what those words meant. His mother and whoever was driving always dodged the question. By the time he'd pieced together what it meant, he'd heard umpteen rumors about who did it, how they did it, and why they did it. Until that last time, when that butthole said those words were about his own mother. His cousin Brett swore it was true. He ground his teeth.

"I can't," Squint said. He bowed his head. Shadows engulfed his face. "I almost didn't make it back from that one."

Pud slumped. He gnawed a fingernail. He sipped his beer. The breeze carried Squint's lingering odor, something like burnt to fuck popcorn, to Pud's nostrils. He gagged, but managed to hold his gorge down again. He brought the can back to his lips. Everybody would freak out if they knew. Nobody would believe him, unless …

Squint says, "And you can't tell anybody"

Pud sputtered beer. He fumbled out his last pack of Marbs. He flubbed the first two flicks of his Bic before he got his cigarette burning. He took a shallow drag and said, "How did you keep this a secret all this time?"

"I got a reason for getting you out here tonight."

Pud peered at Squint, who squinted so hard that he had flattened his eyes and crumpled his forehead down to a wrinkly mass. Pud's mouth dried. He knew he shouldn't have come out here alone with Squint. If anybody found out … but they'd been hanging out little by little over the last few months, drinking with other dudes, ever since most of their classmates had moved to find jobs or gone to college, and anyways, free beer, but now, *fuck*!

"See," Squint said, "pretty soon, I'm gonna change forever. I can feel it coming."

Pud tried to think of something to say. He swallowed some warm beer.

"I don't know for sure how much time I got left," Squint said. "But I know it ain't much." His pain-wracked sigh made Pud shiver. "I want you to put me down."

"No."

Squint's chin dipped. He bared his teeth. Pud dropped his gaze to the frayed hems of his own faded jeans and the holes mottling the canvass of his high tops.

"You owe me," Squint said.

Red scalded into Pud's cheeks and forehead. He tried to meet Squint's hardass stare but he couldn't hack those flinty gashes. He studied the grass and the dirt. Squint wouldn't tell. He wouldn't dare. He scraped his teeth against each other crosswise. *Yes*, he would. Squint had nothing to lose and everything to gain by telling. But all these years, he'd taken more shit than he had to.

"The only hard part is the gun," Squint said. "I can get one, but you have to put it back. I got a way for you to do that."

Pud brought his cigarette to his lips and inhaled an acrid blast of burnt filter. He stubbed out the gross butt and lit up a fresh smoke.

"I already dug the grave," Squint said. "In a secret place nobody will ever find."

Pud exhaled a disjointed series of puffs. The tobacco helped to kill the residual stink lodged in his nostrils. He took another drag and snorted the smoke out of his nose. Squint had to be joking. This whole thing, one big joke. His next toke produced a smooth exhalation.

"As far as my family will know," Squint said, "I ran away. As far as everybody else goes, I just disappeared. Happens all the time."

Pud nodded. Dudes did just up and leave, happened all the time. Just got sick of this goddamned shithole, jumped in a car, and booked without telling anybody. Pud figured he would have done it himself by now, would've done it right after graduation, if he had a damned car. Start over somewhere far away, where nobody knew him. But he was stuck here.

"I'll come get you tomorrow," Squint said.

"Tomorrow?" Pud refocused on Squint's wrinkled brow, his slashed eyes, his set jaw … Squint was dead serious. *Fucking-A.*

"If you can't pull the trigger I'll do it myself," Squint said. "But I need somebody I can trust to bury me, so nobody will ever find me."

Pud shot to his feet. A headrush staggered him. He regained his balance. He rasped, "You're goddamned serious."

"I'd rather you do it, though. I'm afraid I'll chicken out at the last second, or fuck it up, end up in the hospital. That would be a fucking disaster."

"I could fuck it up. I could end up in prison."

"Nope." Squint shook his head. "All you gotta do is keep shooting."

"Somebody could hear, come check it out."

"Not at the place I got picked out."

Pud stammered. He latched onto the first thing he could think of. "What about your family? They're gonna come around looking for you, asking after you."

"Nobody's gonna think to ask you. We've hardly hung out since … you know."

Pud hung his head. Nothing he could say to that.

"I only want to be human," Squint said. "I don't know how much time I have left, but," he cocked his head and widened his eyes, "all I think about is this. I can't stand it anymore. I hate being this … *thing* … that I am. I can't be *it* all the time. I gotta do this before I lose my shot."

Pud shook his head.

Squint lowered his voice while saying, "You owe me."

Sweat prickled Pud's hairline. He did owe Squint, bigtime. He nodded. "Okay, I'll do it."

Chapter Two

The distant squeaks roused Pud from his stupor. He lurched off the living room couch towards the TV. He cranked the dial to OFF, killing the episode of Gilligan's Island. He crossed his fingers against it being *him*. Could be old Barney, their landlord coming to get the little red tractor and hay wagon, or maybe some of the pesticide canisters or propane tanks that he stored in one of the half-dozen sheds that stood aways from the big house.

Pud uncrossed his fingers. He glared at a drawn curtain. The rutted dirt lane would force noises out of most suspensions, but Barney would never allow the engine in one of his vehicles to run hot enough to whine.

Pud let out a growl while taking a swipe at empty air. Two days in and having the run of the house was already fucking ruined. Supposed to be two whole weeks of not having to hole up in his room every morning until everybody was gone, and staying out at night until everybody was asleep. He ought to be putting together parties, and getting girls to come over, instead of hunkering in the living room with the drapes shut, watching the TV with the volume turned down low, and ignoring the phone the few times it rang.

Pud crept towards the entryway between the living room and the dining room. He stopped a few feet back, remaining in the shadowed living room. His angle provided a view of the dirt lane through the western windows. Squint's rusty green Gremlin bobbled along the rutted lane.

Pud slunk through the dining room. He ducked through the sun room, where he suffered the greatest threat of exposure. He backpeddled into the darkened kitchen. He just couldn't see himself gunning Squint down. But he did owe the little fucker.

Pud winced as he gnawed his index nail to the quick. He reached for the knob of the laundry room's door. *Fuck* he owed the little fucker. The fingers of his left hand brushed his lips, but before he could go to work on those nails, he flicked his hand away from his mouth. He'd been up the whole goddamned night trying to figure a way to talk Squint out of it. He'd come up with exactly dick. He needed more time. That's all.

He grasped the knob and placed his palm against the rickety door. He pulled while applying gentle pressure against the door, a trick he'd developed to muffle the noisy shudders of the swollen wood gouging against the bottom of the frame. On the other side he reversed the process. He backed up until he butted against the clunky old washer. He padded across the thin carpet. The concrete beneath the carpet returned a soft slap with each step.

A metallic *chunk* carried to the laundry room. Fuck. Pud went up on his tiptoes for the last few scuffs towards the door to the garage. He eased the door shut behind himself. He lingered on top of the riser. Two steps down, an obstacle course of junk cluttered the garage floor. He was supposed to clean up this crap, his punishment for getting out of the family's two-week camping trip.

He inhaled a hit of dust-choked air. The onset of a gigantic sneeze stormed into his nostrils. He pinched his nostrils. He doubled over and squelched the massive explosion down to a mere spastic bob.

From the front door, *bam bam bam*. Pud had scurried down the riser to the cement floor before he knew it. He halted, but his sneaker toed one end of a curtain rod. The bump set off the broken rod into a spin against the gritty concrete. He lunged down and stilled the rotation. Bent over, he froze, one palm pinning the rod, the other planted in a gummy oil stain to keep himself from falling flat on his face. His heartbeat machine-gunned in his ears. His silent, deep breaths drew in faint gas fumes, which agitated his hangover-queasy stomach.

The front door shunted open. Squint hollered, "Hello."

Pud straightened up and leaned toward the house proper. He cocked his head. Squint's tromps thrummed towards the living room. Pud reduced his breathing to the shallowest, quietest inhales. The slightest twitch of his body seemed to disturb the air as loud as cymbal crashes. He felt like he was suffocating, just like always.

Squint hollered again. Pud's eyelids fluttered. He spiraled below all the times, *so many times*, to the first time … damned if Squint wasn't the first. Clear as day, he saw on the morning *after*, Squint trudging up the sidewalk of the house his mother'd rented three places ago. He'd ducked into his bedroom closet. He recalled the faint chime of the empty hangers he'd bumped. He breathed the same shallow breaths, tasted that stale air. The stiff fabric of his clothesline-dried shirts abraded the back of his neck and bare forearms as he melted into them.

He blinked back to the garage. He clicked his molars against themselves. The day *after* … that's when it all started. Of course he'd quit track and field. Didn't go out for baseball again. Stopped going to school dances. His grades plummeted, hell, he'd barely graduated. He trod over this well-worn ground, ground he'd scrutinized and refined during the excruciating spans between laying his head down on the pillow and actually falling asleep.

Squint's footsteps thudded out of the living room. Pud bent his knees. He probed for a soundless path through the maze of junk littering the cement.

Squint thumped up the stairs. Pud's jaw slackened. Maybe Squint would book after he found the upstairs empty. Pud swept his damp bangs out of his eyes. He took advantage of the distance between the interloper and himself to sneak a few deep breaths.

Squint's footsteps drummed a sulky beat until they stopped dead at the foot of the stairs. Pud pictured Squint doing his hardest squint, mulling it over. Pud scrunched his eyes shut and tried to will the jerk to leave. As long as Squint didn't catch him, afterwards, they could go on pretending like he hadn't been home. But if Squint caught him, he might get so pissed he'd tell …

Pud narrowed his eyes. He thought he detected a sly rustle in the kitchen. *Fuck*. Pud snaked through the jumble of junk. He grabbed the side of the knob-less outer door. A splinter stabbed into his palm. He clamped down on a reflexive hiss. He swung the door wide enough to accommodate his sideways step. He reset the door in its familiar cockeyed position.

He shaded his eyes against the harsh sunlight. He crouched and scuttled through the front yard. The tall grass swished against the hems of the jeans. The glare off the sunroom windows defied his attempt to scan the house's interior. At least Squint couldn't have spotted him before. When his soles hit the dirt lane, he remembered the unobstructed view from within the house. His stomach flip-flopped. He swallowed back the rising bile. He launched into a sprint towards the old grain station.

Tiny spurs, flecking the worn metal rungs, bit into his palms. His first footfall produced a dull clang. His jaw tensed. He slowed to a painstaking pace. He clamped his teeth against the impulse to scurry up the ladder.

A gust flapped the hem of his tee shirt. Almost two stories below, fractured bricks and jagged stones conjured a jack-o'-lantern grin that seemed starving to snap his spine. He forced his eyes away from the drop. He'd gained more ground than he'd thought. Only a dozen or so rungs separated him from the slender catwalk that circled the rusty tank. He permitted himself more speed. Squint shouldn't be able to hear the soft thunks while invading the house.

He scrabbled up through cutout in the catwalk's floor. The thin metal sheeting dipped under his weight. He mashed his back against the tank and edged his way around until the bigass empty cylinder loomed between him and the house. He craned his neck until he could one-eye the front door.

Squint stepped outside, clutching a crinkled brown paper bag that had to contain the gun. Sunlight gleamed off his gelled and parted hair. The breeze ruffled his loose black button-up shirt, which matched his black pants and shiny black shoes. Pud winced. Squint meant to be buried in his Sunday best.

Squint stared at the front door. His back hunched. His free hand squeezed into a fist. Pud bet that the little dude was squinting his ass off. Squint shook out his fist into a open hand. His tight hunch spread out into a loose slump. *Relieved.* He had to be.

Squint gave the house a last once-over, his gaze lingering on the upstairs windows. He got into his Gremlin and guided the beater through a cumbersome U-turn. The Gremlin wobbled along the dirt lane towards the road.

Pud exhaled. Maybe given a little time, Squint would change his mind. Maybe if he ducked Squint long enough, the little dude would come to his senses.

Pud inched along the catwalk to keep an eye on the Gremlin. Another car crested the hill. Its hanging muffler screeched and threw up sparks against the road. The car's Bondo and red body teased Pud's recollection. The car rolled to a stop in front of the dirt lane. Squint got out of the Gremlin and walked up to the red car's driver-window. Pud grunted. The car belonged to one of Pud's older brothers, or cousins, or some leecher who crashed in that rundown old farm of theirs. Squint gestured towards the house. Pud ground his teeth. The little fucker was spilling his guts.

Chapter Three

A remote creak, maybe from as high as the roof, froze Pud. He expected them to come from the trees surrounding the house. He held his breath. Heartbeats careened by while he braced himself for another hint of a mutant paw, while he braced himself for what seemed like the millionth sneaky noise since the sun set.

Just the old house settling. He slumped into the nook between the couch's arm and backrest. He swatted the empty cushions next to him with the aluminum bat, which created a soft *whap*. He dropped the bat and seized the butcher's knife from the coffee table. He stared at the clock mounted on the opposite wall. The darkness obscured the slim minute-hand, but the hour hand stood a notch away from four. He placed the butcher's knife on the coffee table. He rubbed his knuckles in his dry and stiff eye-sockets. He picked up the cold aluminum bat and swatted the cushions again.

He murmured, "Why?" Blabbing wouldn't do Squint any good. Unless ducking him had pissed him off so much that he said 'fuck it' and sicced the whole lot of them on his 'friend.' And if the pack didn't get the job done, nothing would stop the little fucker from telling everybody *everything*. A ring-around-the-rosy of cruel laughter echoed in his skull. He bent his neck. He pressed his shoulder into his ear until his muscle kinked.

Pud straightened his neck and lowered his shoulder. Maybe Squint wouldn't blab, but if he insisted on going through with this dumbass plan, his family were sure to put it together, and then they would attack.

Pud closed his eyes. *After*, he could take Squint's car and go someplace new, where nobody knew anything about him. Everybody would think the two of them said 'screw it' and just booked. He opened his eyes and scoffed. The Gremlin might get him twenty miles away, tops, before that beater broke down for good. *For good.* For better or for worse, no, fuck that, definitely for worse, he was stuck right the fuck here.

His eyelids drooped. He scrunched them down and tried to open them wide, but he couldn't get them all the way up. The only way they wouldn't come after him is if everybody knew about them. But nobody would believe him. He still couldn't believe what he fucking saw. If he told, people wouldn't just whisper behind his back, they'd laugh in his face. He hefted the bat. He wished he had that damned gun.

Pud smacked the bat across the cushions. He should've walked to town before the sun went down. He would've taken the tracks instead of the highway, so there'd be no chance of Squint's Gremlin rolling up on him. But between the trees and cornfields, he would've been a sitting duck for the pack for pretty much the whole six miles, even in broad daylight.

A scrape from atop the roof provoked the image of sharp claws on shingles. Could be a branch grazing the house … *fuck that*. He wasn't gonna sit here on the couch like a moron.

He stole to the basement door. The deadbolt's heavy *clack* made him feel a little better about the thin door. In the pitch dark, he felt for one of the two-by-fours he'd propped on the landing. He butted one end of the board against a crossbeam and wedged the other end against the upper panel of the door. He angled another plank between the stone wall and the lower half of the door. He contorted between his makeshift buttresses. He crept down the stairs, creating a zigzag through the obstacle course of overturned paint-cans. If they got through the door, the cans should trip them down the stairs. He patted the basement's pointy rock wall. They'd break their necks or bash their brains out, either way was fine by him.

He hurried around the old workbench, so that the dusty hulk shielded him from both the kitchen and outside doors. He skipped over the other weapons, every tool with a sharp edge or a blunt end he could find out in the sheds, and went straight for the gassed-up chainsaw. He lifted it by its front hand guard and let it sway to and fro. The chainsaw's lethal aura calmed him. He slipped his hand into the trigger guard. He stabbed the blade into a shaft of dim light that filtered through the basement's filthy windows. The oiled teeth gleamed. He let go of the trigger and fingered the ripcord's handle. So long as they didn't change back into humans, so long as they didn't have guns, he figured he ought to be able to scare them away just by revving the saw at them. If they didn't run … he gritted his teeth. He'd cross that fucking bridge when he came to it.

A glimmer of clean starlight caught his eye. He frowned. A gap separated the hinge of one of the cellar doors from the top of the concrete wall. He pointed the saw towards the busted hinge. Might have been that way and he just didn't notice. He might have done it by accident, while pulling the doors flush and slapping a padlock on their handles. Or a fucking *weresquirrel* might have done it while squeezing inside. He should have tested the doors. He should of tested them from the inside. He chomped his teeth.

Claws skittered against the concrete floor. Pud's recoil turned into a fluke jerk on the ripcord. The chainsaw's engine roared. The saw's teeth grazed the wooden surface of the work bench. The blade's sideways skid bucked against his hands. He tightened his grip and charged around the workbench towards the nearest impression of motion. The chainsaw's teeth tore into flesh. A squeal preceded hot blood spattering a crooked slash from his chin across his nose and between his eyes into his askew bangs.

The blade sprang into open air. Pud spun, screaming, brandishing the chainsaw, hitting nothing. Encroaching dizziness slowed his whirling to a stop. He panted. He scrutinized the darkness for any sign of the enemy. The chainsaw roared. He revolved one more time. *Nothing*. He killed the chainsaw.

The undertones of the engine persisted in his ears. No claws on concrete penetrated the muffled silence. He staggered to the wall. He groped the cold stone until he found the switch. He flicked on the overhead bulb.

He scrunched his eyes shut, then opened them. The blue guts, the brown fur, the red blood reconciled into a rat carcass. A huge rat, but not a shredded weresquirrel. No weresquirrels, no nothing, lurked in any corner.

He breathed out a shuddery, "Oh fuck." He turned off the light. Stiff legs hampered his walk to the cement steps. He placed the heavy chainsaw on a riser. He pulled the ajar door all the way down. He descended to the bottom of the stairs. He picked up the chainsaw. He fixed his stare on the busted hinge. He slotted the ripcord between his fingers. He bared his teeth. They knew exactly where he was now.

Chapter Four

The *snick* of Scott's lighter started a chain reaction. Other dudes holding their own packs passed smokes to Kevin and Terry. The collective smog of the six of them wafted toward the swings where Pud inhaled the secondhand fumes. He just couldn't work up the nerve to bum another one. He squeezed the chains suspending his swing. He toed the dirt, spurring the hard wooden board under his ass into a modest sway. The creaky swing carried him towards the dudes monopolizing the merry-go-round, then away, and back again, and still nobody offered him a cigarette. Maybe if he sidled over there, somebody would just hand him a smoke. His left eyelid twitched. That would be too fucking weird.

Pud glanced toward the sun. Had to be close to seven. Probably less than an hour before he had to start walking if he wanted to make it home before dark. He scanned the dudes. He could try to glom onto one of them, crash at one of their places, but that only happened after getting wasted. The town had already settled into weeknight death. Between the seven of them they couldn't scrape together enough cash for a six pack. If anybody was holding so much as a roach, he wasn't about to share. Chances were that, like most nights, not a goddamned thing was gonna go down. He'd end up starting the long walk after midnight, after Squint and his family had plenty of time to suss out his whereabouts and prime themselves for the perfect moment to pounce.

Bighead Terry exhaled a giant cloud of smoke, which drifted past Pud, then he said, "Remember when Denny stole those pizzas …"

Pud fixed his gaze on a flat gray stone stomped into the faded dirt as he hipped a slight twist into his back-and-forth lull. Everybody knew that story, they'd all told that story about a million times. So the dudes were gonna swap the same tired stories, hoping that beer or pot or whatever would fall into their laps. He stifled a yawn. There were about a zillion Denny stories, the goober always getting skunked on cheap beer and then doing something crazy. Denny had racked up something like a dozen DUI's, his license revoked ages ago.

Pud jammed his sneakers' heels into the dirt and jerked to a stop. Any random batch of Denny stories would include one or two guest-starring Ham, Squint's older brother. Pud furrowed his brow. If he could sidetrack the conversation into Hambone stories, maybe one of the guys would let something slip about weresquirrels. He couldn't be the only one that knew. Maybe everybody knew, but was too scared to talk about them. *Maybe.* He just had to figure out a way to hint at the subject without fucking himself, because if he *was* the only one who knew, and he told, and it got back to the pack, then …

Pud clucked his tongue. He relaxed his brow. That time Ham tried to tip one of Old Man Royce's cows was perfect. By some miracle Ham had made it to the woods without an ass full of buckshot. Pud waited for the fakey laughter to die down. "Hey," he said, "what about that time Hambone tried to tip a cow?"

Nobody seemed to notice. "Hey," Kevin said, "remember that time Denny's cousin wore that bikini?" A couple of long, low whistles introduced the played-out riddle about how the same family tree produced stunted and malformed Denny as well as that blonde babe. The dudes transitioned to the topic of girls. Pud let out a silent sigh. His heavy eyelids drooped.

Somebody mentioned Shanda. Pud opened his eyes. Ol' Hambone had gotten himself caught peeping on Shanda. That time too, Ham had fled into the woods. Twice, Ham had pulled off a miraculous escape. The endings of the two stories might do the trick, might make somebody ask how Ham, who could barely walk without tripping over his own two feet, could possibly manage two great escapes.

Pud croaked, "How does Ham keep getting away?"

Nobody took the bait. His voice came out too broke, nobody must've heard him. Or he'd jumped too far ahead, he should've started at the beginning, not at the end of the story. He caught a snippet of Scott's comment about Brie's gigantic boobs. Pud could compare Brie's boobs to Shanda's, say something about how Ham got a good look, say that Ham would know, say that Ham ran away. Pud lifted his chin. He cleared his throat.

Randy giggled. He blurted, "I like boobies." The dudes laughed their asses off.

Pud bristled. They were so fucking stupid. He squeezed the chains as hard as he could, then loosened his fists. The laughter didn't die, instead grew into that dumbass chant, "I like boobies." He hated himself for buckling under, but he mouthed along. He had to play along, he could get things back on track, back on Shanda, maybe say, 'I like Shanda's boobies.' He winced. That was too stupid. He needed a joke, something good to get their attention. Then he could guide them back to Ham.

"Ass ain't half bad neither," Scott said.

They all cracked up. Pud, under his mimed laughter, huffed out hot air. He didn't know why he bothered to hide anything, since nobody gave enough of a fuck to even glance his way. *Stupid*. He'd wasted too much time overthinking it. Any dumbass comment would've worked. The inevitable 'Ass ain't half bad' chant clarified and its volume grew. He mouthed the words while checking the houses surrounding the park. Anybody within earshot must think the dudes were a bunch of morons, a bunch of jobless, girlfriend-less losers, and he was the biggest fucking loser of them all.

"Sunny's got the best ass," Scott said. "No contest." Scott's claim touched off a heated argument about asses. Pud squeezed the chains until his fingers hurt. He wanted to snarl that not a fucking one of them had even a ghost of a chance with any of the girls they were rating, even if every single contender wasn't already long gone, to college or wherever, getting the fuck out of this bunghole as soon as possible. He couldn't bring up Shanda's ass. The dudes would butcher him, and he'd never get in another word edgewise. He snapped his teeth together.

The ass debate made the typical progression into listing all the babes the dudes claimed to have banged. Pud closed his eyes. He had to work to get them open again. The dudes, every last one of them, were lying. They all knew each other was lying. He snapped his teeth together again. He dipped his chin in order to hide his grimace. He just couldn't do it. They would put up with each other's bullshit, but they might call him out, might blab to everyone that he was still a virgin, or worse, they might … he flexed his cheekbones. He just had to keep his mouth shut and suck it up until their dumbass stories came all the way around again.

He launched his swing into a terse arc. He conducted a mental rehearsal of the links from Shanda to Ham peeping, then Ham skedaddling into the woods, both times, which could prod at least one of the dudes to hint that there were things such as weresquirrels.

He jammed his heels into the dirt, bringing his swing to a dead stop. *Fucking stupid.* Nobody, if they knew, would ever in a million years admit it. Even if everybody knew ... he permitted himself a quiet snort. Nobody knew. If even one person had found out, it would've gotten all over town by now. He could hardly believe it and he'd seen it with his own two eyes. He couldn't say a fucking word.

Scott muttered, "Los Bastardos."

Pud's mouth soured. He spiraled the swing towards the highway. *Keep going, keep going, keep going* ... the shiny white Trans Am turned onto the parkway. Rock from the lamest FM station rattled the tinted windows. *Keep going.* The Trans Am cruised past the dudes' parked cars. Pud breathed out half a sigh. The Trans Am swooped towards the curb and parked long-wise across three parking spaces. Pud twisted the swing until the TA blurred out of his periphery.

Somebody groused, "Fucking bogarts." Pud let the swing untwist. The dudes, hell, everybody, hated Los Bastardos. The two of them got out of the Trans Am acting all cool, like they were trying to do it in slow motion. The posers froze for a second, contemplating the sky from behind their dark sunglasses. The breeze rippled their red and white mesh basketball shorts and tank tops. Everybody else stuck to tee shirts and jeans, but Los Bastardos didn't want anybody to forget that they had started on the varsity team. The dudes had gone quiet. The Bastardos strolled toward them. Pud realized that the dark sunglasses disguised their stares. He dropped his gaze to the dirt between his ratty, off-brand sneakers.

The Bastardos' greetings to the dudes seemed muffled, far away. Pud eased the swing to its lowest point. He hunched. Pud increased the pressure of his clamped teeth. Any second now, they would shift to that familiar, assholish tone and cut him down. Sloppiness slurred the edges of their attempt at funky slang. Pud risked a peek and spotted the fingerprint-greasy silver flask in Dean's palm. The sunglasses pretty much guaranteed that they were baked too, but no way were they about to turn anybody else on.

A series of metallic pings and fleshy smacks accompanied the Bastardos' climb up the monkey bars. Their clumsy footholds and handholds meant that they were more wasted than Pud had thought. They perched high above but within spitting distance of Pud. His hunch stiffened.

"Hey," Greg said, his drunken shout carrying throughout the park, "you guys hear about the big party?"

Pud kept his eyes trained on the dirt. None of the dudes bit, but lighters flicked, and breathy drags agitated Pud's own growing nicotine-fit. Scott, at the tail end of a satisfied exhale, said, "Nope."

"Out at Earl's," Greg said. "Saturday night. Kegger. Pig roast, the whole shebang."

Pud frowned. He hadn't heard a thing about it. He'd been laying low since Squint showed him ... His head shivered, disintegrating *that* image. He focused on the grunts of the dudes, who sounded like they hadn't heard about the kegger either.

Dean slurred worse than Greg when he said, "Everybody's comin' back from school. Everybody."

Pud flinched. That 'Everybody' had to be aimed at him. The Bastardos hadn't ripped into him yet, they were taking their sweet time, waiting till his guard was down before announcing that the giggling assholes were coming home from college, that an unofficial class reunion was gonna go down at Earl's big party. What Dean was getting at ... was that somebody told him the truth. Pud's stomach contracted. He compressed his lips and gagged against the burp that fizzed up his throat.

"Five bucks a cup," Greg said. "I guess that leaves you out, eh Pud?"

Dean laughed his ass off. At first Pud thought that Dean's hee-haws had drowned out everybody else, but none of the dudes even smiled. Pud dropped his own fake smile.

Greg's eyes flicked back and forth. His vibe turned buddy-buddy while saying, "Just kidding, Puddy." A little dickishness returned to his voice as he said, "I'll float you the five, if ya need it."

Pud gave Greg a tight and toothless grin as he shook his head.

"I bet you're real psyched to see your pals," Dean said.

Pud ground his teeth together so violently that his jaw popped. The Bastardos cracked up. Blood burned into Pud's cheeks. Sweat broke out on his forehead. Nobody had ever come so close to saying it out loud ... He tried to sink into complete stillness, hoping that a Zen-like state might cool his face. His skin grew hotter. Tears jiggled on the lower rims of his eyelids. If he cried in front of these motherfuckers, in front of everybody ...

A whisper, from the opposite the side of the Bastardos, reached his ears. "*Pricks*." None of the dudes had joined in the fun. His deep breath started shaky but ended strong. His voice came out cold and hard, as he said, "Just like always ..." his first words steadied him, and a colder and harder pitch issued from deep in his chest while he said, "... I bet nobody'll be psyched to see you bastards."

The dudes' rowdy roars coaxed a chuckle out of Pud. Dean jumped to the grass. Pud straightened his spine. He swung an inch forward and centered his weight on the balls of his feet. He'd never stood up to Los Bastardos. He remembered when the shit all started, fourth-grade bullies picking on a second-grade runt. He doubted he would catch up any closer to them, size-wise. He'd never been in a real fight before. He was probably about to get his ass kicked, but he was so fucking *sick* of it.

Dean's attempt at a cool landing went sideways. His knees kept bending until his ass hit the grass. He bonked the back of his head against a crossbar. The collision knocked his sunglasses crooked. The dudes laughed so hard that Kevin fell off the merry-go-round. Pud's smile showed teeth. He remained on the swing, but poised, ready if Dean kept up his bullshit. Dean used the bars to jerk himself up to his feet.

Below the dudes' howls, a rumble drew Pud's eyes toward the street. A rusty red beater cruised parallel to Pud. A half-dozen pairs of evil eyes glared at him from the darkness within the junker. Pud's smile curdled. A stray shaft of sunlight strafed the car's interior and revealed scalps showing through dirty blonde hair. The more dirty than blonde of Squint's family. A whole fucking carload of Muellers. The dudes' seemed to pay them no mind. Los Bastardos were too busy trying to get back their swagger. The beater crept towards the intersection at the corner of the park, where its chassis rattled for what felt like forever before the car scuttled onto the cross street. The beater's undercarriage scraped asphalt all along the way, the ear-grating scratches marking the car's progress even after the Community Center blocked it from view.

Pud swallowed a wet burp. Greg stood behind Dean, who brushed the dirt off his stupid practice jersey. Dean's unblinking glare lasered in on Pud. He might be able to take the drunk bastard, and the dudes would probably keep Greg from ganging up on him. But then right afterwards, everybody would jet in case one of the park's neighbors called the cops. He wouldn't have time to glom onto anybody. All the Muellers would have to do is wait him out, get him later, or when he tried to walk home. He snarled. He wasn't chicken. He just had to get the hell out of there.

Pud bounded up from the swing. Dean backed up half a step. Pud couldn't prevent his elated growl. He shouldered between the swings, jangling the chains, and he headed towards the strip of grass between the chain-link fences. He flicked his eyes to his right, his vision skimming the gopherhole-ridden soccer field. He ought to have heard that beater's engine, if the Muellers were circling the block. They could've pulled over and fanned out on foot. He had to hide.

Dean called out, "Pussy!"

Pud shifted his gaze to the fence on his left. He stared at the artificial blue of the public pool's water. He pricked his ears for any sound of Dean pursuing. If the bastard did, he'd hold on until the very last second before spinning around and smashing his fist into the dumbass's face. Each step dialed down the Bastardos' insults and chest puffing. Pud imagined the dudes' disappointed expressions. He gritted his teeth. His face reheated. *Motherfuckers.*

He accelerated to a trot. The knobby soil under the sparse grass jabbed his feet through the worn soles of his sneakers. At the corner of the fence he dodged left. The Bastardos unleashed a burst of laughter. He ducked his head and jammed his hands into his front pockets. *Fuck them.* He followed the chain link to the Community Center's outer wall. He entered the narrow walkway between the event center and the post office. The crowded buildings reduced his view of the block across the street. He figured the tight passage would do the same to anybody spying on him.

On his right, the Community Center withdrew, creating a shady nook. He checked behind himself. The coast was clear. He slipped into the gap between the red brick wall and the cluster of shrubs. He squatted behind the largest shrub, his back to the nook's corner. Cigarette butts, smoked down to the quick, littered the brown bed of dead needles.

A whiff of ammonia permeated the char of generic tobacco. Pud palmed his mouth and nose. He took shallow breaths. Little kids and drunks alike used this hideaway as an open-air bathroom. Despite the stench, he could just stay right here. Maybe if he stalled long enough, Squint would change for good, and he wouldn't have to deal with this shit at all anymore. And Squint would never be able to tell.

Trembles pulsed through his torso. He closed his eyes. The Bastardos seemed to know something. The ring-around-the-rosy of toothy grins emerged from his inner darkness. Their laughter intensified his shakes. He opened his eyes and stared at the shrub, at its ugly green needles. He clenched his fists and his teeth until the shakes went away.

He loosened his hands and jaw. Maybe he could explain to the Muellers that he intended to talk Squint out of this crazy plan. Maybe Squint would come to see this as a good enough payback. He extended his fingers, stretching the soreness out of them. *No.* They would still come after him just because he knew. *Goddamn Squint.* Always ruining his life.

He whispered, "Fuck." He couldn't just stay here. The Muellers might ask the Bastardos which way he went and they'd be sure to figure it out. He peered through the shrub. Despite the restricted scope, he eyeballed the entirety of his backyard route out of town. He'd prowled that trail so many times, but usually under the cover of darkness.

He crept out from behind the shrubs. *Play it cool.* He tried to keep his stride breezy, he tried to hide the sweep of his gaze. He had to suppress the urge to bolt across the street. He didn't see a soul. He didn't detect a sound of civilization, not even from the dudes who sat only half a block away. *Dead.* Might as well be a fucking ghost town.

He angled away from the graveled alley. He crossed the street's sun-baked asphalt. He forced himself to slow his pace. He scuffed over the sidewalk and sidled between the small green house and the old savings and loan building. Reentering shady cover reminded him to breathe. Now he only had to worry about somebody poking their head out their back door and yelling at him for cutting across their lawn.

He hurried over the dirt alley behind the buildings. He trespassed through another yard. His shoes whisked into the ankle-high strip of grass before the railroad tracks. If he hooked to his left he could be home in six miles. But the Muellers would figure it out. All they had to do was take the service road and they could run him down in minutes.

He crossed the tracks. He strayed a bit toward the west to a line of stunted trees. He stopped and caught his breath in the polluted grove, which separated the town's dump from a pasture. The grove, in its middle, bulged towards the dump. He stared at the powdery remains of the campfire. Seemed like nobody had bothered with this hideaway for ages. Crunched beer cans and empty booze bottles, their labels peeling or dissolved or both, poked out of the underbrush surrounding the dirt clearing. He supposed that somewhere in the debris lied that empty bottle of blackberry schnapps from his first time. He could hide out until the morning here. He'd have to ride out one gigantic nicotine fit. And if they found him, they could trap him, and do whatever the fuck they wanted.

He waded through the high weeds to the fenceline. He used the lumpy boles and branches to boost himself over a sag in the top line of barbwire. He traced the tapering treeline, traveling under the thinning shelter of the canopy while rustling through the pasture's thigh-high grass. The spans between trees grew. He halted at the last one before the creek.

He hunkered. He performed a slow swivel of his head. Going by fields and pastures would be a major pain in the ass, but he couldn't see how the Muellers could track him unless they got ridiculously lucky.

He froze. Across the river, through the trees, he spotted a smudge of rusty red on the trestle bridge spanning the muddy stream that fed the creek. He stuck to the tall weeds while stealing towards the river bank. The creek's babble didn't overcome the faint putter of a mistimed engine. He bit down on the sides of his tongue. Didn't mean it was them. Just about every dude he knew was a shitty mechanic.

He slunk along the bank until he gained a direct line of sight through the weeds and the trees. The rusty red beater vibrated on the bridge. The passenger door opened. The passenger scrunched forward. Two guys scrambled out of the backseat. One dirty blonde loped to the end of the bridge and skittered into the foliage. The other dirty blonde went to the other end and disappeared into the trees. Both coming towards him. The beater lurched towards the road into town.

Fuck.

He whirled. He kept low while wending through the chest-high stalks. He imagined giant squirrels, tearing through the weeds, their four paws propelling them so much faster than him, freakish squirrels pouncing on him and dragging him down in the brush. He rose into a dash. He shredded through clumps of dry stems and canes. He crashed to the treeline. They wouldn't dare come into town, not like *that*. He stuck to the trees, warding off the thin, eye-level branches with his forearms. His threshing, and his ragged breaths, overwhelmed any sounds of pursuit.

A stitch erupted under his left ribcage. He pressed his left palm against the ripping sensation. He used his right hand to vault himself over the sagged line of barbwire. He labored through the grove. He slowed as he crossed the tracks. He massaged the inflamed tissue under his ribcage. They couldn't jump him now.

He trespassed through the first backyard. The stitch kept him from sucking in enough air. He curved onto the alley that ran along the backends of the Main Street buildings. After passing the crisscrossing alley, he stole a look behind himself. He hustled on a diagonal from the edge of a crumbling lot to the diner's corner. He ducked into the cranny between the bankrupted diner and the fire station.

He inhaled the musty, gritty blend of the fire station's cinder blocks and the diner's rain-rotted wood. His shoulders grazed both walls. A few steps in, where the sun never shined, the temperature plummeted. He shivered. His sneakers' toes nudged crumpled cigarette packs and candy wrappers. He caught his breath. His right elbow scraped brick. He overcompensated to the left and mashed into spongy wood. He pivoted until his shoulders didn't touch either wall. He stared at the rusty backside of the Salvation Army donation box that blocked the street-side opening. He could sit down with his back against the big metal container. They might never find him. Or they could trap him and murder him right the fuck here.

He clambered over the donation box. He fretted along Main Street. Nobody else peopled the sidewalks. The 'closed' sign hung in the corner market's entrance. The laundrymat's glass windows showed no one. Not even the garble of TVs drifted from the open windows of the block's second-story apartments. The deep hush could tempt them to try to take him down right in the middle of town.

He crossed his arms over his stomach. *They wouldn't.* At least not in broad daylight. Nighttime, though, was another matter. He had to find somebody to hang out with. A hook to the right would take him back to the park, but he couldn't face *them*, not after seeming to run away with his tail between his legs. He jaywalked the street and turned left at the corner. The slaps of his soles against the concrete sidewalk disturbed the quiet of the shady residential area.

Four blocks down, at the T-intersection marking the eastern border of town, the rusty beater appeared. Pud jumped. He bolted across the street, his instinct propelling him south against the beater's northward heading. He darted into the alley and sprinted the block to the highway. On the other side he vaulted the triple-wire fence. He ignored the pulsing threats of another explosive stitch. He battered through dry cornstalks. The dust and chaff forced a wracking cough out of him. He realized he might as well scream, 'Here I am!' along with his commotion.

He tried to slow down, but he couldn't. The corn went on forever to his left. They might be right on his heels, flanking him, surrounding him. He accelerated. He burst out of the corn. He skidded to a stop on asphalt. He whipped himself around in a full circle. Endless corn to the east, about three blocks of town left in front of him before more fucking corn for-fucking-ever, and them somewhere behind him. He pivoted to his left, towards Main Street.

The clattering of a thin metal against pavement paralyzed him. Somebody gunned a gas pedal and an engine produced a series of mistimed bangs. The rusty red beater rumbled into view, cutting off Main Street.

Pud raced into the nearest backyard. He skidded around a garage and flattened his back against its dirty white wall. The beater's racket loomed. He choked down the impulse to run. That's what they wanted, to flush him out, for him to run right to the edge of town. He zeroed in on the back porch of the next house. *Baker's house.* Sophomore year they'd started filching beers from the old fridge in the back porch. If Baker's old man ever caught on, he never cared enough to lock the back door.

He rushed to that porch. He held his breath outside the screen door. The blasts of beater's engine swamped any sounds from the house's interior. He peered through the screen. No lights as far as he could see, all the way into the kitchen. He thumbed the catch on the door's handle. He pressed until he felt the catch *click*. Unlocked. He glanced towards the street and spotted the beater. *Good.* They wouldn't know he was sneaking inside the house.

He opened the door. The hinges' squeal made him cringe. He inched the door shut behind himself. The beater's racket faded. He detected the babble of a television, maybe from upstairs. He guessed that Baker's dad wasn't home, or the downstairs TV would be blaring. From somewhere high, muffled by walls and floorboards, Baker's mom called, "Is somebody there?"

Pud tensed. Timid footsteps creaked down the stairs. Pud swayed towards the screen door. His eyes fixed on the gap on the far side of the old yellowed fridge. With each of the three steps, he extended his legs as fast and as far as he could, but hesitated, and lowered his shoes with the lightest touch he could muster. He settled into a tight crouch between the unpainted wall and the fridge.

Baker's mom lingered in the kitchen. Pud imagined the frazzled little woman listening hard, maybe a little freaked out. If she came out and found him, he didn't have the slightest fucking clue what he would say to her. The smooth soles of slippers scuffed linoleum, away from him. He didn't move until she padded all the way back upstairs. He slumped. He stretched his legs out in front of himself, trying to make himself comfortable. He figured he might be here a while.

Chapter Five

Pud stubbed his toe against a hard rut in the service road. His stumble kicked up splinters of petrified mud. His gritty skid to a halt set his teeth on edge. He swiveled his head. He steeled himself for shouts, for thumps of sneakers and combat boots, and *paws*. The breeze rustled corn leaves. The thick darkness revealed only an outline of the nearest stalks on the other side of the railroad tracks.

A sudden yawn threatened to unhinge his jaw. He squatted down to stretch out his tired thighs and tight hamstrings. He groaned throughout his shaky upward thrust. His legs felt worse. Hunkering down on Baker's back porch had knotted up his muscles something fierce. The long walk home had just about finished his legs off, not to mention his low back and feet.

He spotted another ridge in the service road. He kicked the ridge, spattering dirt against nearby weeds. *Fucking Squint*. He wouldn't be here right now if not for him. He could just kill the little butthole. His stomach cramped. He had to … if he didn't … The cramp sharpened, doubling him over. He moaned. His moan drew a wet burp from deep, deep down. He clamped a palm over his lips and scrunched his throat.

He focused on relaxing that cramp, sneaking air through his nostrils, ratcheting up out of his clench an inch at a time. When he reached his full height, the cramp had abated enough to permit him a heavy sigh. He hung his head. Squint must have told them *everything*. The cramp withered to mild pulse. He curled his fingers into fists.

The cramp flared. He squeezed his fists into tight balls. The ragged rims of his chewed-up fingernails mashed into the meat of his palms, but he knew they wouldn't break the skin, wouldn't draw blood, never had since … He swallowed against a gag. He gurgled, he strained, he gained ground. He released his fists and shook out his fingers. He let out a series of weak coughs. His stomach muscles slackened.

The big party. He see-sawed himself into a rigid march. His legs stiffened with each step. His feet kept sliding forward within his loose sneakers, smashing his sore toes into the narrow rubber tips. He glowered at his only pair of shoes. The frayed hems of his faded jeans flopped in his peripheral. His *best* jeans, his only Levi's. The college kids would have the latest stuff. His shitty pants made his one polo shirt look ridiculous. His tee shirts weren't any better. All of his *peers*, every single one, would make fun of him. No way in hell was he going.

He chewed the sides of his tongue. Everybody was gonna be there, though. *Everybody*. For sure the Muellers would pick that night to come looking for him. There would be no witnesses. They could get away with anything they wanted. That pukey taste oozed up to the back of his mouth. Unless he wanted to spend the night hiding out in some pasture or field, the only safe place in the world for him on Saturday night was Earl's party. He fucking had to go.

On his right, on the other side of the tracks, the spiky contours of the frame of the old milking house emerged from the darkness. The starless night blotted out the rest of the burnt-down farmstead. He exhaled a shallow sigh. The last bend lied dead ahead. After that, about a half mile or so to home. *Home*. Where *they* might be waiting.

He drifted toward the rails. He waded into the stone bedding, his shoes clicking the arrowhead-like rocks into each other. He could camp out somewhere in the ruins of the farmstead. He hadn't roamed the place in years, having grown bored with exploring the destruction long ago. He stared into the pitch blackness. He tried to remember some cranny that wasn't absolutely filthy. Had to be way fucking worse now. His own bed was more or less clean.

A headache gathered over his eye. He winced. His gums throbbed. Through gritted teeth and sealed lips, he growled. He was dying for a smoke. His mother had forgotten a full carton of her lady cigarettes. He'd starting scissoring them down to Marb length, and putting them in an old hardpack, but he'd seen right away that shit wouldn't fly. He hadn't been able to think of another way.

He twisted his arms over his stomach and squeezed until the worst of the nicotine fit passed. His eyelids drooped. The burden of his head strained his neck muscles. The wind ruffled corn leaves. They must have figured that he was spending the night at Baker's house, they must have given up by now.

He trudged towards home. He meandered away from the tracks' stone bedding to the quiet dirt of the service road. He dropped his arms to his sides. The ache in his gums subsided to a buzz. As soon as he chainsmoked two or three, he would scarf down a super-sandwich, settle his stomach. He yawned. Then he would lock and barricade his bedroom door, and sleep until he couldn't sleep anymore.

He rounded the bend. The distant orange light at the intersection of the road and the highway limned the curve of the grain station's tank. He picked up the pace. A little ahead, from the weeds on his left, a dull clink disturbed the silence. He stepped back and lowered himself into a slight crouch. He raised his fists. His stomach muscles seized. He gaped, unable to catch a breath while the seconds bled out.

Two scrawny shapes slouched out of the weeds. *Muellers.*

The first one gripped a baseball bat one-handed, trailing the bat's end in the dirt behind himself. When he neared the railroad tracks, the half foot of chain lanyard bolted to the end of the bat jangled against the stones. The other Mueller rested his bat over his shoulder. The lanyard bolted to that wooden club swung to and fro. "Sneaky fucker," the first Mueller said, "ain'tcha?"

Pud juked toward the weeds. Both Muellers lurched to cut him off. Pud sprang the other way. He hurdled the tracks and sprinted homeward. Somebody shouted, "Get that cocksucker!"

Pud found another gear. His tortured toes went numb. He rehearsed his simple plan, the house, the basement, the chainsaw. The house the basement the chainsaw. House basement chainsaw …

He caught a whiff of a noxious odor. His next breath drew in a stronger dose of the musk. The next forced him to retch, runners of bitter drool exploding out of his mouth and sticking to his cheeks and chin. The impression of Squint's monstrous mutation warped the edges of Pud's sightline. He skittered. One ankle bone clipped the other. He yelped. His weight yawed to the right, too far in front of his feet. His shoes skidded into stones. He sprawled. Flinty edges lacerated his palm and rent the knees of this paper-thin jeans. His left elbow smacked into the steel rail. His cut and bruised limbs kept struggling. He wrested himself upright. He vaulted back into a sprint.

Their uncoordinated stampede rattled rocks far enough behind him to give him hope. On his right, swishes disturbed the tall grass before the fenceline. Behind him, somebody growled, "Fuck!" A powerful wave of body odor choked Pud. He lunged his leg to keep from outrunning himself again.

The crashing through the tall grass surged almost abreast of him on his right. The stink intensified. He glimpsed, through the thick grass, an oily black eye, and the glint of crooked orange teeth. The swishes passed him. They meant to cut him off. A fire kindled in his lungs. He couldn't suck in enough air. The stitch erupted under his ribcage. The white-hot agony spoiled his stride, which devolved into a gimpy lope. *I'm gonna die!*

He planted a heel in the stones and skated to a stop. The freakish hulks kept plowing through the tall grass. He stooped and groped until he found a stone the size of his palm. He hurled the chunky stone at his human pursuers. One of them performed a herky-jerky, last-second duck. Both slowed to a cautious approach while readying their baseball bats.

Pud fixed his eyes on the dangling links of chain as he felt for another good rock. He listened for the monsters somewhere behind him. He hand grazed a railroad tie and bumped into a spike that jutted out far enough for him to wrap three fingers around its length. He yanked the spike out of the splintered tie. He grasped the dull tip of the heavy spike between his fingers and thumb and flicked it towards the Muellers. The spike flipped end over end, and *thocked* the closest Mueller square in the forehead. The Mueller folded to a knee. His dropped bat clattered across the rails. He sunk down to his stomach. The other Mueller stopped dead in his tracks. He knelt beside his fallen kin.

Pud snapped his teeth twice. He scooped up stones and whirled, strafing the tall grass, flinging stones so hard that the force hurt his shoulder, but he growled through the pain, spinning, peppering the humans, then wherever he sensed the monsters lurked, while ranging back and forth to score more ammunition. He located a hunk of coal almost as wide and flat as a Frisbee. He slung the uneven disc at the tall grass. A deep thud preceded a squeal. That pained cry fueled Pud. He disregarded the size of projectiles, mixing in a few pebbles into his frenzied barrage.

He reeled toward the humans. The railroad tracks' emptiness stretched into the darkness. He wheeled and charged into the waist-high grass. He leveled brutal kicks at the thickets he believed might hide the weresquirrels. He struck nothing but foliage. They were gone.

They were gone.

He tossed back his head and howled at the black sky. His howl persisted until he went hoarse. He wrenched his head back down and slapped his palms on his bent knees. He sucked in ragged breaths through his savage grin.

He caught his breath. The breeze rustled through the corn. His grin twisted into a grimace. They hadn't bothered to hide their secret from him. For sure Squint must have told them everything. For sure, they were hellbent on murder. He might have lucked out and fought off four of them, but next time the whole pack would be coming. He launched into a jog towards home. He would need a fuckuva lot more than sticks and stones.

Chapter Six

Pud palmed the cherry of his lady cigarette so that nobody would spot him crouching in the corn. He took a last drag and stubbed the smoke out among the dozen or so littering the dry soil between his sneakers. He settled on the rusty pump-handle as a landmark in the yard between the big old farmhouse and the barn, so he could locate his nicked up baseball bat in the field. He would want the Bluelight Special if he had to hoof it home.

He tapped his index finger a few times on the top of his pack of cigarettes. He could smoke another, but his throat was cashed. He should just walk out of the corn and up to the house, like he'd gone into the corn to take a leak, like all the other dudes, like he'd been partying all along. In the house he would find an abandoned cup he could wash out. Nobody would suspect that he hadn't paid the five bucks or whatever. He would play it cool, say his hellos to the clusters of classmates across the yard, and stroll right into the long, low barn. He'd tap himself a cold one while pretending to dig the lameass pop music. The savor of the roasted pig wafted out of the barn over the cornfield. He licked his lips.

His eyes blurred over the cliques cluttering the yard, but he still registered the bright new clothes, the slick hairdos, and the gleaming smiles. Their chatter could only testify to how great college was, or how much money they were making. He chewed on the sides of his tongue.

He eyes kept focusing on Los Bastardos. Maybe the combination of midnight darkness and their stupid sunglasses would keep them from seeing him. He shook his head. No way he'd get that lucky. Not with them sitting on top of the picnic table and facing the corn. No doubt they had picked their perch so that nobody yo-yoing between the house and the barn would escape their bullshit. They would want revenge on him. They would announce to everybody that he still lived at home, that he didn't own a car, that he didn't have a job. After they made fun of his shitty clothes, they might try to kick his ass.

He pulled out another slender cancer-stick, then slid it back into the pack. He could sneak around front and avoid them entirely, but then he would have to face Earl, who stood guard while charging cash for cups. He didn't think his blistered and bloody toes could take the walk back home. Anyways, the Muellers were out there, somewhere. He rubbed his palm against his forehead down to his chin. *Fuck them.* He would worry about that shit tomorrow.

The last two dudes rose from the picnic table, leaving the whole damned thing to Los Bastardos. All the girls had bailed a long time ago. Pud couldn't help a hard smile at how everybody either dodged or ditched them. *Fuck it.* If he could fight off two goons and two monsters, he could handle Los Bastardos.

Pud ambled out of the corn. For good measure, he faked zipping up his pants. He angled towards the house. From the corner of his eyes, he fixated on them. He exhaled a shallow breath. He shook out his arms and shoulders. He simulated a casual pace. He needed one step to lose sight of them when Dean's slurring cackle turned his head. The beer sweats had collapsed Dean's fancy hairdo and greased his face. Alcohol-bingeing had crossed his eyes. "Well, well, well," he said. "Fuck a fuckin' duck! Fuckin' look who fuckin' showed up!"

Greg snorted. He raked a hand through his damp black hair. Pud doubted that the bastard knew he'd made a ridiculous rooster-comb on top of his head. Greg said, "Thought I smelled chicken shit!"

Pud faced them. He stared at Greg, then at Dean. He cleared his throat and said, loud enough to carry throughout the backyard, "See you guys are sitting with all your friends."

Dean launched himself off the picnic table. Pud sidestepped his clumsy charge. Dean stumbled into a headfirst dive. His momentum outstripped his struggle to get his hands underneath his fall. His chin hit the ground and he scudded across the grass.

A bystander squawked. Other witnesses tittered. Greg staggered to Dean, who shoved away his best friend's attempts to help him up. Grass strains streaked Dean's brand-new jeans and polo shirt, and a thick green stripe slashed on a diagonal from the corner of his chin to lips.

Pud shrugged. He pivoted towards the house.

Dean sneered, "Gonna run your ass away again."

A hand snatched the hem of Pud's tee shirt. Pud twisted. Greg yanked on Pud's shirt, stretching the material so much that the collar throttled Pud's Adam's apple. Pud wrenched himself free. He tee shirt hung in a weird shape almost down to his knees. He balled his fists and ground his teeth.

Dean lurched to his feet. He snarled, "We are gonna beat your ass to shit."

Greg and Dean advanced. A crowd formed around them. Pud saw nowhere to run and no rocks to throw. He slid a step backward. They were gonna kick his ass, *bad*.

Greg grinned. He said, "Unless you get on your fucking knees …"

Dean barked a cruel laugh. "That's right," he said. "In front of fucking God and fucking everybody, cocksucker!"

The crowd's nervous chatter died to silence. Pud's face went nuclear hot. He steeled himself for a kamikaze lunge.

"Oh my god! John Everson! How the hell are you?"

Pud's head twitched. He couldn't reconcile his real name with the voice. Only his family used his real name, since forever. He blinked. He took longer to reconcile the long brown hair and sunken cheeks, and the drab long-sleeved tee shirt and black pants with Tommy, his former classmate, who used to dress all GQ over a buff bod. He scrutinized Tommy's smile, but couldn't detect any sarcasm, or any meanness at all.

Tommy held out his hand. Before Pud knew it, they were shaking jive-style. Pud couldn't work up a single word to greet one of his old tormentors, not one who was treating him like an actual human being. Tommy looked at Los Bastardos and said, "What's going on here?"

"None of your fucking business," Dean said.

Tommy's smile faded to a grim slash. He stepped into Dean and Greg's space, forcing them both to step the fuck back. He said, "I'm making it my business."

"Lordy, lordy, lordy! What we got goin' on here?"

Pud bristled. He had no trouble recognizing Kevin's assholish voice. Just like always, the overgrown redhead had cut the sleeves off of his tee shirt to show off his veiny biceps. Nothing but cruelty deformed his snaggly grin. Under his caveman's brow, his too-small eyes jittered. Pud gnashed his teeth. It had all been fucking Kevin's idea in the first place, he had gotten all the others to go along …

In Kevin's wake, in all their jocky glory, their tee shirts boasting their various colleges, the rest of the fucking assholes, clutching cups of beer and smirking, swaggered towards Tommy.

Kevin threw one of those rippling arms around Tommy's shoulders and said, "We got ourselves a problem?" Kevin kept smiling, but his tiny eyes stilled. Kevin's followers crowded out the onlookers and half-circled Greg and Dean, who retreated a couple of more steps. Los Bastardos muttered while fading into the other partygoers. Kevin crowed, "I didn't think so."

The others laughed their asses off. They all seemed to notice Pud at once. Somebody slapped Pud on the back, some called him 'Pud,' others called him 'Puddy,' and Matt, his hairline having lost another inch or so since graduation, mischief dancing in his eyes, slapped a Vartz in Pud's hand. Pud regarded the bottle. Everybody else held plastic cups, but the cold bottle's cap felt tight, felt un-tampered with. His gaze skipped across each of them. He caught no signs of anticipation, no hint of a setup. *Fuck it.* He cracked the cap, tipped the bottle, and guzzled half the beer in one pull. He wiped his mouth with the back of hand to hide his grimace. Didn't matter how cold Vartz got, still tasted like shit. His former classmates cheered his gusto. He couldn't help smiling.

Tommy shook a cigarette out of his pack of Marbs and offered it to Pud. A frown flickered over Pud's face. Tommy hadn't smoked in high school. Pud took the cigarette. Tommy pulled a Zippo and lit the cig for Pud before touching the flame to his own. Pud inhaled a huge hit. He exhaled a gray cloud that was equal parts smoke and sigh.

"It's really good to see you John," Tommy said.

Pud nodded. Tommy's obvious sincerity choked him up a little, but he managed to rasp, "You too, man." The tension melted out of his jaw and neck. His stomachache vanished. He raised the cigarette to his lips.

A hand whapped him on the back. The impact jarred the cigarette from his fingers. The sting made him arch his back. The cigarette hit the grass and threw up sparks. Kevin bellowed, "His name's Pud!"

Pud coughed. He knelt down to pick up the cigarette. Kevin muttered something behind his show of teeth. Pud regretted kneeling. He got the gist, even if he couldn't make out any of Kevin's words over the rowdy laughter of the others. He glanced at Tommy, whose eyes seemed to sink into their sockets, their light gone dead. Pud popped up and away from Kevin's immediate reach.

"Why are you so late?" Matt said. "You walk all the way out here?" A tingle ghosted through Pud's earlobes. Matt used to love to sneak up from behind and flick his earlobes so hard they turned red. A couple of times Matt's claws had drawn blood.

"Nah," Kyle said. "His girlfriend gave him a ride." Pud took great care not to look down on short Kyle, whose shoulders and chest seemed broader and thicker than ever. Kyle had always reminded Pud of a human rottweiler. Kyle didn't usually pick on kids, but when he backed one of the others, everybody knew to keep their mouths shut and eat whatever shit the assholes saw fit to dish out.

They all busted a gut, except Tommy, who brushed his hair from his forehead, revealing a deep vertical crease between his eyebrows. Pud clamped his teeth on his tongue. He crossed his fingers that Matt still drove the same shitbox as in high school, and blurted, "Least I don't drive a station wagon."

Matt glared at Pud and said, "What college you go to again?"

Their laughter's previous buddy-buddy vibe soured. Pud shifted his eyes from one side to the other. They had surrounded him. He contracted his fists, then forced himself to loosen his hands. He shouldn't have opened his big mouth. That had only ever made them madder.

"Must be matriculating somewhere," Trent said. "Check out that shirt, that has to be part of a fraternity pledge." *Trent.* He always looked like he was having the shittiest time, unless he was picking on some poor underclassman. Counting from the very first one in third grade, string-bean Trent, with Kyle standing behind him, must have inflicted about a hundred pink bellies on Pud alone.

"More like a sorority pledge," Matt said.

Pud flinched. He caught himself fussing with his shirt, and forced himself to stop. Nothing worked, anyways. Los Bastardos had stretched his shirt out so much that it might as well be a goddamned dress.

"You borrow that from your mom?" Trent said.

"Come on now, leave poor old Pud alone." Rich said. Rich's blonde spikes gave him a couple more inches of height. His braided rattail draped over his left shoulder and curled just below his neck. Pud could never look at the asshole without remembering that time in the fifth grade when Rich had stabbed him in the back. Shoplifting had been all Rich's idea, but he had been smart enough to stand lookout. He played dumb when Pud got caught stuffing a candy bar in his sock. After a while, Pud got to thinking that Rich had narked him out just to see him get caught and banned from the store.

"Maybe you and Puddy wanna be *alone*." Matt said.

The others hooted. Rich shook his head. "Nah," he said, "everybody knows Pud gets off on having an audience."

Moisture sheened Pud's eyeballs, distorting his vision, reducing their faces, and everything else, to blackness, except for their bright white toothy mouths. Coming here had been a mistake. All his presence would do, all his presence *could do*, was remind them of one thing, and the beer and the booze and whatever else they were on would make them mean enough to tell everybody every fucking thing. He ground his teeth. He clamped his hands into fists, which he raised towards his face, but he had a premonition of a bawling baby rubbing tears out of his eyes. He stared at the grass between his feet. His hands and his jaw went limp, his knees loosened. A pang stabbed through his swelling bladder. He crunched his guts to stop himself from pissing his pants. Somebody was gonna say it, somebody was gonna say it … His voice husked through his dry throat and mouth as he said, "The Muellers are weresquirrels."

His revelation calmed their laughter. His heartbeat pulsed all the way through the throb in his bulging bladder. The next beat intensified the agony. He braced himself for the worst.

They roared. The heat in his cheeks dropped from scorching to boiling. The tears cleared from his eyes. Their faces regained definition. They laughed their damned asses off. Matt had even flopped onto his back, holding his belly as he rolled back and forth. The pressure in Pud's bladder abated.

The tail end of Pud's deep breath snared the barest whiff of burnt popcorn. He whipped his head back and forth. Beyond the ring of his tormentors, close to the cornfield, Squint leaned against an oak's trunk. He squinted so hard that his forehead crinkles seemed to stack underneath his thinning bangs all the way to the top of head. The surge of pressure in Pud's bladder forced him to hop from one side to the other, but still a squirt escaped. *Oh fuck oh fuck.* They were gonna kill him for sure now.

Kevin whooped. The big redhead hollered, "Well looky the fuck here!"

The others turned towards Squint. Trent sprayed a mouthful of beer. They all busted out laughing. *Fuck. They all* were here. Pud shuffled backwards, then to the side. He scrunched his stomach to stall his brimming bladder. There was nowhere to run.

Squint shoved himself off the trunk and uncrossed his arms. He strode towards the circle. His squint mellowed a few notches, but a couple wrinkles lingered over the V of his eyebrows. He switched a brown lunch bag from his right to his left as the others handshaked him into the circle. All their smiles strained far past any semblance of friendliness. Squint didn't smile at all.

"Uh-oh Puddy," Kevin said. "Squinty don't look happy with you!"

Squint ignored Kevin and held his thousand-yard stare on Pud. The heat rushed back into Pud's face. He tried to return Squint's stare, but after a second he dropped his gaze to his threadbare sneakers. The increasing tension in his jaw and neck spoiled his attempt to strike a casual pose.

"You should'a heard what Pud just said," Matt said.

Pud raised his eyes. Squint cocked his head to the side. Pud studied Squint's expression. Squint was pissed, no doubt, but Pud didn't see any sign of the apocalyptic rage he expected.

"I need to talk to you," Squint said. "In private."

Pud's head slumped. Squint had to have heard. He'd been standing right there.

The assholes harmonized a jeering 'Oooooh' as Squint grabbed Pud by the arm and pulled him out of the ring. Pud jerked his arm free. Squint glowered at him. Pud closed his mouth. The assholishness of their former classmates didn't seem to bother Squint one bit. Squint nodded his head towards the field and started walking. Pud took a pull off of his Vartz and followed Squint to the edge of the corn. He glanced back. The assholes sauntered back towards the barn, the beer, and the music. Probably to talk their shit to everybody.

"You owe me," Squint said. "Where the fuck have you been?"

Pud sputtered. He said, "What the fuck do you mean where have I been?" Pud searched Squint's face for a clue. Squint's eyes narrowed, as if he didn't know a goddamned thing about his kin's attempted murder. *As if.*

"Fuck it," Squint said. "We're here now. Take this." Squint held out the crinkled paper bag.

Pud shifted from foot to foot. He took the bag. The heavy metal threatened to tear through the bottom. Pud groaned.

"Careful with that," Squint said. "It's loaded."

Pud palmed the bottom of the brown paper bag. If he adjusted it just right, he could pass it off for a pint of booze. He frowned. There was no way that Squint would give him a loaded gun ... unless he didn't tell his kin anything, unless he didn't know they'd been stalking him. Pud said, "Ah ... so you still want to go through with this?"

"Why wouldn't I?" Squint waited for an answer. He squinted. "I got everything ready. Question is, are you ready?"

Pud compressed his jaw. He nodded. "I gotta piss," he said. He hurried away from Squint.

Chapter Seven

"This old place looks exactly the same," Tommy said.

Pud studied the collapsed roof of the forsaken farmhouse. He'd never known that Tommy dug taking long walks on the country roads and exploring all the abandoned farmsteads. Pud scraped his shoe on the dirt lane. The painful flare forced him to draw in a sharp breath. His blistered toes screamed bloody murder. But Tommy had wanted to 'ramble,' for old time's sake, and he had invited Pud, and despite the agony he was glad he had tagged along, because Tommy was the one person who hadn't bragged about how fucking great college was. So far every moral of Tommy's stories had been that the whole thing sucked pretty hard.

He re-rolled the top of the brown paper bag for the umpteenth time. The worn creases didn't even make any noise anymore. Not like the countryside around them. Every little rustle through the weeds, every hint of a snapped twig or scuffling in the soil, reminded him that *they* were out there, somewhere. Watching, waiting for just the right time to pounce. They probably thought that Tommy would ditch him, eventually, a thought that had crossed his own mind a time or two. Or maybe Tommy was leading him into a trap, and Kevin and the other assholes were hiding inside the farmhouse. Pud affected a single shake of his head. He had scrutinized Tommy, and he just didn't get that kind of vibe. Something was different about Tommy, other than the longer hair, the lost weight, and the somber clothes, but Pud couldn't quite put his finger on it.

A droplet splashed onto Pud's cheekbone. He flinched. A volley of sprinkles hit his face. *Rain.* He sighed. The cloudburst startled the thick canopy of the farmstead's overgrown trees and pelted the sunken roof.

"Come on," Tommy said. He jogged to the front door of the house. Pud followed, the first few pigeon-toed steps creating bursts of pain, then his feet went numb. Tommy shoved the front door, which produced a woody shudder before opening. The entrance's mustiness scratched Pud's throat and dragged a harsh cough out of him. He trailed Tommy into the kitchen. A long, low wooden table dominated the room. Somebody had removed all the doors from the cupboards. Dust coated the bare shelves, counters, and the tabletop. The roof appeared intact and still waterproof. Pud stared into the dark doorway to the house's interior, but he detected no movement, and no sound except the steady patter of the rain.

Tommy propped himself against the sink and produced a joint. He glanced at the paper sack, *again*, but he still didn't ask. He flicked his Zippo. The flame exposed the dark bags under his eyes, and the lines in the hollows of his stubbly cheeks. After a couple puffs, Tommy got the joint going, took a hit, and held it out to Pud. Tommy had gnawed his fingernails down to a few jagged spurs above the quick.

Tommy leaned back against the warped counter. "Squint sure seemed happy tonight," he said.

Pud snorted. He took a big drag. Last he saw Squint, Big Cindy had been all over him on Earl's living-room couch.

"Sure," Tommy said, "Cindy's no prom queen, but she's a nice girl."

Pud shrugged. He'd gone to school, he guessed all the way from kindergarten, with Cindy, and he couldn't remember either one of them ever saying more than two words to each other. "I guess I never really knew her." He passed the joint to Tommy.

"Yeah," Tommy said. He toked. While holding his breath, he said in a shallow tone, "Kind of funny, isn't it?" He exhaled, gave the joint to Pud, and said in his normal voice, "You sit in the same room as somebody for pretty much your whole life, and you don't know them at all."

Pud nodded. He took a hit off the joint because he couldn't think of anything to say other than, maybe, 'This is the most you've ever talked to me too.'

Tommy's voice came out hoarse while saying, "I'm sorry man."

Pud exhaled. The darkness obscured Tommy's stooped face except for the sagging corners of his lips and the black holes of his eye sockets.

Tommy's voice hardened as he said, "I should've stood up to Kev and the guys earlier. I meant to. But when it came down to it, I was a coward. Again. Like always."

Pud held the joint out to Tommy, who had hung his head, and didn't seem to notice. Pud shifted his weight to the other foot. He retracted the joint. He took another drag, just to do something, anything.

Tommy raised his chin. The darkness didn't obscure the wetness of Tommy's eyes. Pud handed him the joint. Tommy accepted it. He crossed his free arm over his chest and clutched his bicep. He waved the joint like it was no more precious than a cigarette. He said, "I'm flunking out, man."

The rotted wood and crumbling plaster returned a lone flat echo of Tommy's confession. A rush of mustiness cut short Pud's sniff. He opened his mouth. He closed his mouth.

Tommy barked a parched laugh. "Thought it would feel better to admit it, to say it out loud, but it doesn't. Fuck." He took a hard drag that burned about half of the remaining joint to ash. Tommy passed the roaching joint to Pud.

Pud muttered, "Sorry, man." He grimaced. He puffed on the joint to keep from saying something else stupid.

Tommy's exhalation came with a long "Phhhhhhhh." The cloud of his secondhand smoke hazed the kitchen. "The only class I even bother to show up for anymore is Existentialism," he said. "Just can't seem to get out of bed to go to the others. Seems so fucking pointless."

Pud held his hit while holding the roach towards Tommy, who waved it off. Pud had reached a nice level of toastiness, but there was another hit or three on the roach. He fought the expansion of smoke in his lungs.

Tommy crossed his other arm over his chest. "I've been thinking about it," he said. "Fuck, it's about all I think about, the way I treated people like you, like Squint, like Cindy, and just about everybody else that wasn't in my clique." He looked Pud dead in the eye and said, "I'm so fucking sorry."

Pud tamped the roach out on the side of the old wooden table. He didn't know what Tommy wanted him to say. He mumbled, "That's okay, man."

"It's not okay." Rain pattered all the way to the floor in a distant room. Tommy said, "It's ruined your life."

Pud blurted, "Squint wants me to kill him."

Tommy stared at Pud. "No shit?"

Pud nodded. He raised the paper bag a half inch, but Tommy whipped out his Marbs. He gave the pack a shake so that a butt stuck out towards Pud, who placed the roach on the table. He took the offered cigarette.

Tommy stuck a cigarette between his lips. He lit Pud's, then his own. He pulled a deep draw. He raked his eyes with the back of his cigarette hand while crossing his free arm over his chest. He said, "Fuck."

Pud nodded. "It's been eating me up inside," he said. "I can't sleep, I can't eat. He's serious. He even dug a grave for himself. I've been ducking him, trying to figure out a way to talk him out of it ..." He peered at Tommy through the smoky haze. Tommy's eyes looked like they had sunken even lower into their sockets. The urge to tell it all trembled through Pud. The Muellers hunting him, why Squint wanted to die, *fucking weresquirrels* ... but, right before the smoke cleared, he thought he caught a twitch at the corner of Tommy's mouth, maybe a trace of a smile. Maybe Tommy didn't believe him. *Maybe.* Maybe he should show the gun. Tommy had been right there when Squint gave it to him.

Pud shifted his grip from the roll to the edge of the bag's opening. The weight of the gun unspooled the bag to its full size.

Tommy murmured, "Fuck." His chin lowered to his chest. He raised his cigarette hand as if he had something to say. He folded that arm across the other one, across his chest.

Pud frowned. Tommy didn't get it. Pud's frown deepened into a scowl. Tommy couldn't be getting it. He could only be thinking ... Pud yelled, "No! You don't get it!" He flung his cigarette straight down against the wooden floorboards and stomped it dead with his heel. "None of you get it!"

"I get it. You got to face the truth man. I'm so sorry for what happened. Nobody should be forced ... I can't imagine how horrible that must have felt." Tommy lifted his face. He opened his arms and said, "Especially in this fucking place, where none of us ever get to be ourselves."

Pud's stomach sizzled. He expelled a faint gurgle. The pain in his guts blazed.

Tommy whispered, "It's okay man."

Pud gnashed his teeth. He gagged back his rising bile.

Tommy raised his voice to a gentle coo, saying, "It's okay man."

Pud tore out the gun. He squeezed the trigger, again, and once more. Tommy slumped to the floor.

"Fuck, man!"

Pud spun towards Squint, who stood in the kitchen doorway. Squint cringed, extending his arms, shielding his face with his splayed fingers.

Chapter Eight

Pud gripped the edge of the sleeping bag and pulled. The effort strained his low back, but didn't budge the zipped-in corpse. He leaned further into the Gremlin's hatchback. He gritted his teeth. He grasped the widest bulge in the sleeping bag. Through the damp polyester, Tommy's slack shoulders made him gag. His outward haul discharged a blast of mustiness into his face. Halfway out of the Gremlin, the corpse's weight seemed to double. Pud grunted. The bag slid. He heel slipped on the mud. He scrabbled to keep his footing. He right hand shifted to a wet spot on the sleeping bag. His stomach flopped. He hoped the earlier rain caused the spot, and not seepage from within.

Squint scurried around to the Gremlin's hatch. He grabbed the bottom of the sleeping bag. He trapped the corpse's legs against his hip. The sleeping bag sagged in the middle, but Pud stabilized his balance and secured his hold. Squint revolved while switching the bag to his other hip. His back to Pud, Squint led the way into the trees.

Pud looked over his shoulder. The Gremlin sat at the dead end of the grassy ruts, nosing an inch over the high bank of a stream. Pud had never booze-cruised out this way. He'd gotten lost about a million gravel roads ago. The Gremlin had jounced over a pasture to find this hidden road, which started off dirt before deteriorating into furrowed grass.

Squint's uneven pace tugged Pud's attention back to their chore. Squint brushed through a patch of giant weeds. Pud cleared the sludge from his cashed throat. First Squint's shoes, then Pud's, squelched on the thin strip of mud twisting through the thorny weeds. The tips of the overgrown stalks tangled overhead. The dense snarl blocked most of the faint glow of the overcast night sky. The sloppy trail snatched at Pud's soles, aggravating his blistered toes and threatening to rip his shoes off his feet.

Squint accelerated. The sudden yank on the corpse caught Pud mid-stride. One foot in the air, his other foot skidded from its ball to its heel. Pud lunged forward, saving himself from falling flat on his ass. The flare of agony from his toes distorted his voice to a sharp whisper as he said, "*Slow down.*"

Squint decelerated to a saner pace. Pud huffed out a hot breath. He didn't know why he felt compelled to whisper. There couldn't be another soul around for miles and miles. He ground his teeth. Even if nobody ever found the body wherever the hell Squint was taking him, there was no way he'd ever be able to clean up all the blood back at the farmhouse. The only thing he could think of was to burn the place down, but that might just bring the cops' attention to it. *Fuck.*

His eyelids lowered until only the puffy bags under his eyes kept them open. *So fucking tired. Stupid.* There was no way they were gonna be able to hide this. He was gonna go to prison for the rest of his goddamned life. Nobody would talk about any fucking thing else. Everybody would want to know why he did it. His vision tunneled down to burden in his arms.

The thicket gave way to trees. Squint snaked between massive trunks. Pud jerked back on the corpse in order to slow Squint down. Pud's hip-torque nudged the gun upward so that the weapon threatened to fall out of the back of his waistband. Pud shifted the weight of the corpse to his left arm. He slapped his right hand behind himself and rammed the gun back down, scalloping a little skin. He winced. He threw his right arm back under the corpse. Squint sped up again. Pud grimaced. He guessed Squint was ready to get it over with.

His biceps and forearms burned. In order to maintain his hold, he had to squeeze the corpse against his ribs. His grimace deepened. He shook his head. He wouldn't give up. He wouldn't cry about it either. He would deal with it, one way or another. He hoisted the corpse. He stiffened his spine. The dead weight scraped down his ribcage to his hip bone and dragged his spine back into a hunch. He couldn't go much farther.

They staggered into a clearing. Squint slowed to a stop. He panted, "I need a break."

They lowered the corpse to the damp grass. Pud surveyed the scattered clumps of trees that stood out in the darkness. Just another asscrack in the hills.

"You ready?" Squint said.

Pud nodded. They lifted the corpse. Squint led the way. After a long while, the dense clusters of trees and patches of tall weeds began to look the same to Pud, to the point where he suspected Squint was lost and was running them around in circles. Pud's second wind withered to fumes. Each step ravaged his toes. He couldn't hold his end of the corpse higher than his thigh. He just wanted to lay down and wait for the police to come take him away.

Squint exhaled an almost silent "Phew." Pud raised his head. They'd reached the banks of a creek. Squint said, "It's easier going from here on out."

Squint followed the stream deeper into the countryside. Pud hustled to keep up. He said, "Where are we?"

Squint squawked a laugh. He said, "Nowhere."

Pud tilted back a tad to slow Squint down.

"I don't know the whole story," Squint said. "But there's some sort of land dispute that's been going on like since forever. Like, over a hundred years."

"Never heard of it."

"Because it's between folks who don't even live around here anymore. Doesn't really matter. What matters is, nobody works the land. Nobody even hunts it, just too far and too hard to get to. Land just sits here. This is where my people go when they … change over the last time."

"You mean …"

"Yeah."

The darkness reduced visibility to near nothing. All that Pud could see, the shapes of massive trees, clumps of dense weeds, even the overhang of the creek's banks, provided perfect camouflage for monsters.

"Don't worry," Squint said. "If they see you, they'll just run away. That's why nobody knows."

Nobody knows.

"There it is," Squint said.

Squint pulled him towards a gigantic tree. The leafless branches stabbed into the sky. A shovel protruded from a mound of black dirt next to the tree. Pud figured the digging must have taken Squint all day. Squint guided them right to the edge of the black hole.

"Ready?" Squint said. "One, two, three."

They heaved the bagged corpse into the hole. A dull splat carried up from the dead center.

Squint muttered, "Fucker deserved it."

Pud flinched.

"Fuckers stole so much from me," Squint said. "From both of us."

Pud clenched his teeth. His vision blurred around the fringes. He lashed himself sideways. He lurched a step away from Squint.

"Okay," Squint said. "Ready?"

Pud squeezed his fist so hard that his knuckles crackled. He couldn't think his way through all the beer, and Tommy's primo weed, and he was so goddamned tired. He shook out his fists. He massaged his jaw until it unlocked. He rubbed the back of his hands over his eyelids. He sniffled. He had the gun. He'd already *murdered* tonight. He couldn't see how he could talk Squint out of it, especially now that Squint could say, 'What difference will one more make?' or 'You owe me more than ever, *now.*' Fucker using *all* of it. Pud mouthed, *Against me.* He mouthed, through his bared teeth, *All of it*!

Pud snatched the gun out of his waistband. He spun. Squint slouched, his head bowed, staring into the muddy hole. Pud sighted the gun at Squint's temple. Pud sputtered a thready whine. He chomped to cut off the whimper. His focus narrowed to Squint's skull. *The little fucker …*

Squint's head rotated towards Pud. Squint's eyes bugged. He ducked and tumbled away from the grave. He shouted, "Whoa!" He scrambled behind the trunk of the massive tree. "What the fuck!"

Pud swayed. His gun arm fell limp beside his hip. His jaw slackened, his lips parted, but he only managed a weak huff.

"Holy fuck!" Squint said. "I meant are you ready to bury him! Don't fucking shoot me!"

Pud's shudder grew into the full-body shakes, which concentrated in his knees, forcing him to bend his legs in order to calm them. He tried to exhale but his empty lungs produced the barest wisp. He gaped, unable to draw in air, then he wheezed in a giant breath. He coughed the back of his throat bloody. Sweat stung his eyes.

"Fuck, man," Squint said. A nervous laugh ended his exhale. "Jesus Christ. I should'a told you already. I don't wanna die anymore."

Pud worked up an echo of Squint's laugh. He spat out, "What?"

"I …" Squint edged out from behind the tree and spread his arms wide "… after tonight, after what happened, how things were, I decided I want to … you know, every second counts now. I can't waste a second anymore. Shit …" He dropped his arms and slumped against the tree. "… I wasted so much goddamned time."

Pud recoiled his head as far back as his neck allowed. The gun slipped from his loose fingers. He fumbled the sweat-slicked firearm back into his grip. He swallowed. He said, "Then get them to stop."

"Get who to stop what?"

Pud stared at Squint. His expression, his *squint*, seemed honest. But Pud couldn't tell in the dark. "You don't know your … family has been coming after me?"

Squint's lips opened. He performed a slow shake of his head from one side to the other.

Pud angled his face toward Squint. "You didn't tell them what you were planning?"

"No! That was the whole point of it!"

"Then how did they find out?"

Squint reeled towards the grave. He bent his face toward the hole and the darkness swallowed his features, but Pud could tell his squint had scrunched harder than ever. "I swear I didn't tell them a thing." He slapped his thigh. "I did go to my aunt, and ask her if she'd put me down. Maybe she told. And then maybe they been watching me all along, saw me change in front of you to prove it. Then they just put two and two together." Squint stared into the muddy hole. He murmured, "Or …"

Pud bit his tongue. He coiled his index finger around the gun's trigger.

"I wish they would go away forever," Squint said.

Pud withdrew his index finger from the trigger.

Squint turned towards Pud. "I'll find out if they know that you know," he said. "If they do, they'll want to be sure that you'll keep your mouth shut."

Pud nodded. "Who'd believe me anyways?" The mocking reaction of Kevin and Tommy and the rest of the assholes flashed through his mind. His cheeks warmed, but he willed himself not to blink in the heat of Squint's gaze.

Squint pointed at the grave. "If we tell them about this, then you guys will be even."

Pud slitted his eyes. He nodded.

"All right," Squint said. He circled the edge of the grave to the mound of mud. He grabbed the shovel. "Let's get this over with."

Pud resituated the gun in his waistband, careful to avoid the bloody gouge. He'd be holding onto it for now.

Chapter Nine

The leaves of the last row of corn chafed Pud's sunburned forearms. He hocked and spat. His hours in the pesticide-sticky fields had built up a toxic scum, which resisted all his efforts to scruff out his mouth. Clearing his throat only made him thirstier.

His knees popped as he squatted. The stalks provided a thin shade from the noonday sun. Beyond the faded green of the grassy strip on the other side of the fence, heat waves shimmered up from the gray highway. He waited out another throb from his busted and blistered toes. Taking the long way around, just in case the Muellers still hunted him, had murdered his feet. He could turn himself in. They couldn't get him in prison. He wiped his index finger under his eye socket. He sniffed. He couldn't claim self-defense.

He scowled. His vision focused until his head ached. Not self-defense, but maybe justified. Maybe. He sighed. He was tired of thinking about it. He was just too damned tired, period, to figure it out. But he had figured out what people would say, if he turned himself in, about *why* he turned himself in. He ground his teeth.

He grunted upright. He unclenched his fists. He shook the feeling back into his stiff fingers. He pushed down the top line of the three-wire fence and straddled his way over from the field to the flat grass. Faint laughter, unmistakably feminine, carried from the few blocks between him and the park. He frowned. Sundays were always the deadest, and he hadn't seen a girl at the park on any damned day, since fucking forever.

He scuttled across the vacant highway. He slowed into the lush shade of the willow and oak-lined sidewalk. He flicked his parched tongue over his lips. The explosions of agony from his toes numbed down to stinging pulses with each rapid step. His approach separated the racket in the park to a bunch of individual voices. Their breezy energy prompted a trace of a bounce in his blister-crabbed stride and invoked the glimmer of a long-lost summer evening. He recalled the squeals from the jam-packed public pool, the car stereos blasting tunes, the rowdy shouts, and himself, practically skipping to the park to show off his brand spanking new white sneakers that he just got for his thirteenth birthday.

He crossed Main Street and sighted the park. If not for the harsh noontime sunlight, he would've sworn that he'd stepped into that remembered night. Cars filled all the slanted parking spots along the street. Somebody occupied every seat, including the picnic tables, the teeter totter, the obstacle challenge, the swings, the monkey bars, and even the grossass sandbox.

He glared past the frayed hems of his faded generic jeans at his tattered sneakers. He raked his fingers through his sweaty bangs. He grimaced. He looked like shit. He felt like shit. He surveyed his former classmates. He scoffed. *Of course.* He should've known every-fucking-body would get together the day after. Squint just fucking couldn't say over the phone, just had to fucking meet in town, and everybody was gonna say, 'Did you see Pud? He looked like death on a Popsicle stick.'

They were all gonna see him whispering with Squint. *Fucking Squint.* He glanced over his shoulder. The prospect of turning back forced his attention to his wrecked toes. All the walking had made his low back sore. Six more miles on foot ... he sighed. The bags under his eyes seemed so heavy that they'd sagged down to his cheekbones. He just wanted to get this over with. Maybe get Squint to give him a ride home. The little fucker owed him that much.

He blinked up some moisture in his irritated eyeballs. He took a deep breath. He willed his stride to normal proportions as he crossed onto the soccer field. His headache sharpened.

A jarring chorus hollered something that sounded like a distorted "Hey!" The lazy revolutions of the merry-go-round panned grins aimed at him.

Too late now. He corrected his course towards the orbiting grins. He strove to maintain his casual gait. His guts squirmed. *Here it comes.* He straightened out of his slight hunch. His spine crackled. He tried out a meek smile before all those even white teeth. Sunlight flashed off the aluminum beer cans in a few hands. A couple of dudes, Hank and Brett, nerds that had taken what passed for advanced math classes with Pud, hopped off the merry-go-round with their open hands extended. Pud halted. He scrutinized their eyes, but he couldn't detect a trace of cruelty. Their smiles seemed like the real thing.

Hank slapped Pud on the back. "We were just talking about the time you told Jane to knock it off." He said. "Remember?"

Pud lowered his shoulders. He breathed a hoarse chuckle. He nodded while shaking their hands. He did remember. Only a dozen students in the room, taking a Calculus test, all of them spread out in anti-cheating formation. Jane, one of the hottest babes in their whole class, so spoiled, so used to getting her way all the fucking time, sitting a couple of desks behind him. Jane whispering for the answer to question three, and him pretending not to hear her, hunching closer and closer to his desktop, trying like hell not to snap his last stubby number-two pencil in half. Jane raising her voice with each whisper, until her voice rose so fucking ridiculously loud that the whole room, including Mrs. Cassidy, had to hear her. Finally, he exploded, his shout turning into a puberty-stricken yodel of "Knock it off!"

Pud's smile quivered, but he managed to keep his lips from twisting. He'd always assumed everybody pegged him as a nark, just another reason for all the kids to hate him. Hank and Brett seemed to think his outburst had been hilarious. Pud didn't see Jane among the gathered alumni.

"I always hated how she always cheated off me," Brett said. "Wish I'd had the balls to stand up to her."

Pud honked.

"No big surprise she didn't show her face," Hank said. "Since she didn't get into college."

Pud flattened his flinch as fast as it appeared, reducing it to the slightest tic. He scanned their faces. Hank and Brett, and the others within earshot, showed no signs that Hank's comment could be taken as a dig at him too. Except that he hadn't tried. Maybe that made all the difference. He tried a smile. His headache descended a notch.

More laughing, grinning dudes swarmed around Pud, and somebody, he didn't catch who, slapped a cold Cherry-Berry wine cooler in his hand. The fruity fizz soothed his cotton mouth. Brett dipped his head towards the frisky girls still revolving on the merry-go-round, and said, "When did they all get so damned foxy?"

Pud's 'Yeah' came in dead last, so far behind the others' that a few fellas raised an eyebrow towards him. He needed to say something, *fast*. His mind lurched back to the last time he fucked something like this up, mostly by fucking over-thinking it, and he blurted, "I like boobies …" He guffawed. Confusion warped their smiles. *Dumbass*. None of these guys had been there. They didn't know what the fuck he was talking about. None of them were gonna finish off his reference. If he didn't do it, he would look like a jackass. He swallowed and said, "… ass ain't half bad neither!"

They all cracked up. Pud tipped his bottle. He used his tongue to limit the stream of wine cooler down his throat. His eyes darted from side to side. He couldn't decipher the spirit of their laughter, but the way they'd drawn themselves into a circle, and so a little away from him, was nothing new.

He lowered the bottle from his lips. He had to find Squint anyways. Hank pivoted towards him and slapped him on the back. Next thing he knew, they herded him deeper into the park. He copped a Marb. The happy chatter bubbled around him. Girls bopped to the radio. His toes didn't seem to hurt so much anymore, even when he went up on their tips to get a good look around. Not just his class, but what seemed like the entire student body from his senior year, had come home and, for at least this afternoon, revived the park. He savored a huge drag off his smoke.

A sudden part in the crowd exposed Squint, who sat on a picnic table's bench. Squint held hands with a beaming Cindy. A bunch of other coupled-up dudes and chicks perched around the lovebirds. Pud's brow furrowed. He'd figured that neither would acknowledge their little grabass session in the sober light of day. Squint, for once, wasn't squinting. His casual expression almost made him … Pud grimaced. He shook his head.

Squint locked eyes with Pud. Squint's eyes narrowed. His forehead crinkled.

Pud raised his eyebrows. He lifted his right hand, the cigarette sending curls of smoke around his upraised palm.

Squint tapped his index finger against the side of nose, twice.

Pud scowled. What the fuck was that supposed to mean? Fucker, all he needed to do was to give him a nod.

Squint turned his smile towards Cindy, who said something to him out of the side of her mouth. They giggled together. Some joker in Squint's immediate clique made a wisecrack and Squint laughed out loud.

The laughter spread to those milling around Pud. His smile felt stiff and fake. He took a couple glugs from his wine cooler. He shuffled towards Squint. He slipped close enough to hear Squint's comical tone. Whatever Squint said made those around him laugh their fucking asses off. Cindy leaned in and whispered in Squint's ear. Pud's stomach cramped. He forced his tongue between his front teeth to relieve the grinding pressure. Obviously the little fucker didn't give a fuck if the rest of the Muellers stayed on the warpath.

"Hey Pudsky, how ya doin'?"

The familiar dickishness in Greg's greeting raised Pud's hackles. He didn't need to turn around to know that the other fuckface was there too. Los Bastardos always traveled together. He faced Greg and Dean anyways. He'd put them in their place once, he'd be glad to do it again, in front of *everybody*. He cleared of his throat to make sure his voice came out loud and strong. "Los Bastardos," he said. "Crashing the party like usual, 'cause nobody your own age will hang out with you."

The few weak laughs died a quick death in the swelling silence. Pud's chin dipped. He glanced past Los Bastardos. A couple high-school girls shook their heads. Pud frowned. They were just too young to know how big of assholes the Los Bastardos really were. They didn't understand that it was fair to call them 'Los Bastardos' because they called him 'Pud,' first. He sought wiser expressions, the knowing expressions of his classmates, who'd suffered like he had. His gaze centered on Cindy. The deep crease between her eyes and her flat lips left no doubt that she disapproved. Squint also observed Cindy's reaction. He hit Pud with a disapproving squint of his own. Pud gaped. He couldn't believe they all were taking Los Bastardos' side.

"Jeez," Greg said. "Harsh, dude."

"Yeah," Dean said. "Harsh, dude."

Other dudes and girls piped in. Pud grated his teeth. He couldn't believe that nobody saw through Los Bastardos' act. Somebody behind Pud muttered, "What an asshole." Pud cringed.

Greg looked past Pud and said, "Yo Squint!" Greg cocked his head. He faked a serious air while saying, "Is it cool to call you that?"

Squint snorted. He went all goony and waved off Greg's concern.

"Lookin' good, dude," Greg said.

Pud brought his bottle to his mouth too fast and sloshed a little wine cooler onto his chin. He disguised his wipe of the syrupy patch by taking a drag off his cigarette, which had smoldered down near to the butt. He could understand everybody buying Greg's phony warmth, but Dean's snaggly smile practically screamed 'liar!' Pud had to give it to them, though. They'd wised up. Telling Squint he was looking good, that made everybody compare the little fucker to him. Might as well be telling him that he looked like shit, except they said it without saying it, without making themselves look bad. *Motherfuckers*!

Dean's snaggle lips wormed apart, baring his wolfish teeth. He said, "Don't Squint look good?"

Pud's stomach cramped. The hush pressed in on him. *Everybody* waited for him to answer. He imagined bashing the wine-cooler bottle straight into Dean's ugly mouth, shattered teeth and glass spraying all over the fucking place. He bit his tongue and shoved that image out of his brain. He had no time to lose, not with everybody staring at him. He willed himself not to look at Squint. Everybody would see that. He could admit it. A tightness deep in his chest slackened. He performed a slow scan of their expectant faces. Everybody was waiting for him to say … *something. Say something*!

He couldn't help stealing a glimpse of Squint, who leaned towards him, also dying to hear what he was gonna say. Pud's mouth ran dry. His next glance at Squint hardened into a glare. Squint squinted, then shifted his eyes toward the grass. Pud's lips twitched. He could confess. It would serve Squint right. Confess to murdering Tommy.

Pud cast his gaze toward the trampled grass too. Somebody coughed. He raised his eyes. Nobody saw the evil behind Los Bastardos' innocent masks, because they were all looking at him. He squeezed the wine bottle in the effort to shift his tension from his face to his fist. He couldn't remember who he was supposed to respond to, let alone what that particular bastard had said.

Pud zeroed in on Dean's ugly smirk. Pud clicked his teeth together. *Fuck it.* "Look around," he said. "We're not little kids anymore." He latched onto a nod from somebody a row deep in the spectators. "You two can't go around dishing out titty twisters and pink bellies anymore." He let the few angry yeahs and nods play out. He puffed his chest a little. "You're lucky we all don't get together and take turns giving you bastards wedgies and swirlies." More remembered. Their grumbles grew louder. Their anger stoked him. He pitched his voice so they could hear him throughout the goddamned park while saying, "You're lucky we don't beat the shit out of you." During the louder responses, he permitted himself a quick survey of the angry victims of Los Bastardos. *Go in for the kill.* He reeled his gaze back towards Los Bastardos, opening his mouth to say, "You're-"

The sweep of his eyes slammed to a stop. At the back of the crowd, Kevin's grim glare rose above the mass of heads. Matt, Kyle, Trent, and the rest of Tommy's crew flanked the big redhead. The looks on their faces felt like a punch in the guts. *They knew.* Pud managed to draw enough air to wheeze, "... lucky your ass ain't already grass."

Pud ripped his attention away from Kevin. He took a backward step. Everybody had closed ranks, there was nowhere to run. He gaped at Squint, whose eyes showed the whites all the way around. Squint's head disclosed a single tremble, which Pud hoped was the tiniest nod he'd ever seen.

Squint stood. "Whoa now,' he said. "Everybody settle down." He hustled out to the middle and stood between Los Bastardos and Pud.

Pud knuckled up his fists. Squint, now the fucking hero. Pud caught sight of Kevin and the assholes jostling their way towards him. His stomach acids roiled up his throat. A hot belch left the sour taste of semi-digested berry wine cooler in his mouth. He took another backward step.

Squint swiveled sideways between the two parties. "Let's everybody settle down now," he said. He squared his shoulders to Los Bastardos, who had gone all redfaced and jutted chins. Out of the corner of his mouth, Squint rasped, "Go!"

Kevin's advance had seemed to tighten the pack ahead of him. Pud slouched and pushed through the opposite side of the crush. He heard Squint's pleas for calm until he reached the cooler air outside of the crowd. He dropped the bottle and ducked into a half-crouch. He circled the fringes of the crowd. He looked over his shoulder. Stuck in the middle, tall-ass Kevin aimed his tiny eyes right at him. Tremors ran from Pud's knees up his spine and chattered his teeth. Kevin looked down. Pud figured that Squint had thrown himself in front of the big asshole.

Pud hurried to the strip of grass between the Community Center and the soccer field. Kevin would see him, but he'd be long gone by the time the neanderthal and his flunkies got out of the crowd. And those rich assholes didn't know a fucking thing about the secret footpaths in and out of town.

Chapter Ten

Pud looked over his shoulder. A wall of corn lined the other side of the highway. On his side, a block behind him, the lazy sway of the vines of weeping willows hid the last house. The foreclosed filling station marked the far end of town. The noise from the park didn't reach this far. The smooth blacktop of the station's front lot soothed his blistered toes, which the cracked concrete and stony dirt of his secret paths had savaged, flaying his gait down to a hobble.

Plywood sheets boarded the filling station's windows. A huge padlock fastened a thick chain through the handles of the dead-bolted front doors. A slight buzz drew his attention to the Coke machine. He licked his lips. He paused mid-step, but he had no money for pop. Sometimes he could work his arm up the machine's slot and jiggle a can free, but he had to get his ass out of sight.

He hustled along the lane to the back lot. He hooked around into the crevice beside the empty ice bin. He leaned against the building's fake brick. The awning's shade cooled him. He surveyed beyond the trees and bushes bordering the graveled parking lot to the fields and green pastures rising all the way up the hill. He had a godawful walk ahead of him, but he'd made it. He could take his time. He knew the location of a couple springs clean enough to drink. And nobody was about to catch him out in the boonies.

He closed his eyes and breathed. Kevin's face materialized against the blackness. The certainty had sizzled from Kevin's furious tiny green eyes. Kevin, and so all his running buddies, knew, *they knew*. Flecks of vomit spurted up his throat but he clenched his entire body, hunching, gagging through gritted teeth, and he forced it back down. He shuddered into a sag against the rough wall. A long cherry-berry wine cooler belch fumed up his raw throat. Sweat pooled on his upper lip.

He croaked, "They know." He'd take it back if he could. He sniffled. He brushed the back of his hand across his cheekbone. The only way to make it right was to turn himself in. *Confess.* He took a hard sniff. The cops would want to know where the body was. They would want to know where he did it. They would want the murder weapon. They would want to know where he got the gun. He couldn't figure out the math that left Squint out of it.

He brushed his cheek again. Squint's face replaced Kevin's against the black backdrop. Squint's grin went all goofy, his eyes all googly, for Cindy. Squint deserved to be all googly in what little time he had left. And he hated to think what might happen if Squint changed for keeps after the cops locked up the poor little bastard. Pud shook his head. There was no way to do it without taking Squint down with him.

Squint's googly eyes narrowed to slashes. His goofy grin *snaggled*, just like Dean's Bastardo smile. Squint had buckled under to peer pressure, taking Los Bastardos' side, just to be fucking cool. Pud clicked his teeth together. So what. He wouldn't throw Squint under the bus just because Squint did it to him, even though the little fucker deserved it.

A bolt of pain jarred his eyes open. He whisked his right index finger away from his teeth. He'd gnawed through to the quick again. He wrapped his left hand around his pulsing finger and squeezed. He hocked and spat. *Fucking Squint.* He guessed it was only a matter of time before Squint figured out he could climb the ladder by stepping on him. All the little fucker had to do was watch Los Bastardos.

He gave his finger a tighter compression. He groaned, then let it go. Los Bastardos had come up with a better way to put him down. He supposed things were only gonna get worse. No way would they forget that he'd made them look like jackasses three times now. Most of the witnesses would go back to college at the end of the summer, but not the dudes.

"Huh." He stared at the fields and pastures climbing up the hill. He could hide until everybody went back to college, including Kevin and his crew. He clinched his chin, between the ball of his thumb and the middle knuckle of his index finger, and lifted his face an inch. He blew all the air out of his lungs.

Rustling disturbed the bushes hemming in the corner of the graveled lot. He thought he caught a whiff of that burnt popcorn musk. *The Muellers*! He launched himself off the wall and slewed towards the lane. They couldn't get him out in the open.

Kevin and Matt blocked his way. Pud skidded on the gravel. He fell on his ass and sprang right back to his feet. Kevin's sleeveless tee-shirt showed off the jagged blue veins marbling his huge biceps. His caveman's forehead loomed over his tiny eyes. Matt's round eyes dropped into a hardass stare.

Pud spun. Kyle and Trent emerged from the bushes. Rich followed them. Pud froze. His heartbeat hammered inside his skull. Trent's sour expression hovered over Kyle's broad shoulder. The heat had wilted Rich's blonde spikes.

Pud pivoted back to Kevin and Matt. He backed up. Kevin's cinderblock fists meant they knew enough. And he'd been dumb enough to lead Kevin and his crew to a lonely place where they could beat the rest out of him.

Kevin waggled his gigantic head. He said, "You think you're slick?"

"Stupid moron," Matt said. "We've been playing Ninja since the fifth grade. We just hung back until you fucked yourself."

From behind Pud, Trent said, "We could murder your stupid ass and nobody would know."

"Or care," Matt said.

They were right. One hundred percent. They'd be on him before he could scream. He back-peddled deeper into the parking lot, away from Kevin and Matt's advance. Behind him, footsteps crunched over the gravel in a semicircle.

"Where's Tommy?" Kevin said.

Pud's trembling jaw stilled. Maybe they didn't know as much as he thought they did. He flicked his dry tongue over his cracked lips. He squared himself to Kevin. He cocked his head. He said, "Why should I know?"

"Why did you run?"

Kyle's icy question compelled Pud to turn around and face him. Pud hoped his sunburn disguised his flushed cheeks. A fingernail flicked his earlobe. He cringed away to avoid another flick. He pressed his shoulder into his injured lobe. Sure as shit that fucker Matt had jumped on the first chance to do it. Probably drew a little blood, just like the good old fucking days. Matt pounced and nailed Pud's other earlobe. Pud staggered away from the asshole. That last flick landed harder. Pud felt hot wetness drip from his ear.

Kevin lunged at Pud. The *smack* made Pud leap backward. Kevin stood still. He held his massive right fist against his open left palm at the level of Pud's eyes. Pud didn't realize that Kevin had clipped him until the tip of his nose throbbed.

Kevin growled, "Answer the fucking question."

Pud sensed the others crowding behind him. Tiny red lines jagged through the whites of Kevin's eyes. Somebody shoved him. Somebody else caught him by the hem of his tee shirt. Another shove ripped his shirt, and another shredded the rest of the threadbare material right off of him. A fist pummeled his shoulder. He raised his arms in front of his face. He ducked his head towards the crooks of his elbows. He took a hard punch to the tricep. Somebody grabbed his left arm and jerked him off his center of balance. He lost his right sneaker while scrambling to get his legs back underneath himself.

Pud wished for the gun, wished he hadn't decided to hide it in his underwear drawer. He spat, "Stupid fucker."

Matt hollered, "Fuck you!"

A boot heel smashed the three littlest toes of his shoeless foot. The agony exploded up through him and he tossed his head back and howled. A blow to his spine thrust him down to the gravel. The sharp stones, the broken glass, and the rusty metal bits tore his palms and skinned his knees.

"Shut the fuck up," Kevin said. "Or I'll knock your teeth down your throat."

Pud clamped his mouth shut. He rocked back on his knees. He wrapped his arms around his torso. He shifted his right foot to raise his broken toes off the ground. He closed his eyes. The bursts of agony made him reel. The color of his closed eyelids darkened from red to black.

"He likes it like that," Rich said.

He cracked open an eyelid. Their crotches surrounded his head. He ducked a little lower.

"Kyle," Kevin said. "Tell him what you told us."

Kyle, his tone low and hushed, said, "Tommy told me he was going to beg Pud and Squint to forgive him. He told me it was driving him crazy."

"I would've told him to forget about it," Matt said. "I would've told him that Pud liked it."

Pud winced.

"Obviously," Rich said.

"Shut up," Kevin said. "Go on."

"Tommy told me he thought about killing himself a lot," Kyle said.

Pud didn't move a muscle.

Kevin nudged him with his boot. "What do you got to say?"

"If you hadn't been such a fucking crybaby," Trent said, "Tommy wouldn't have felt so bad."

Somebody slapped him in the temple. Sparks flew across the backs of his eyelids.

"Knock it off," Kyle said.

Somebody, Matt, Pud thought, grumbled.

"You two left the party together," Kyle said. "Nobody's seen him since."

"Tommy did ask me to forgive him," Pud said. "I could see how it was killing him." Pud raised his head. "He believed he ruined my life." He looked up at them. He closed his eyes. *He did.* "He … did." Tears rolled down his cheeks. "And I got m-mad." He shuddered.

"Then what?" Kyle said.

Pud drew a hitching breath. He wiped his runny nose. "I … I turned my back on him." He sniffled. "I walked away. He tried to catch up to me, but I started running, and I got away from him."

"Fucker."

Pud braced himself for more blows. He shouted, "I was mad!" The blackness behind his eyelids gave way to red. He didn't dare sneak a peek, though. "But after a while, I cooled off. I realized that I was being a dick. I went back, to … to find him, to tell him that I forgave him. But I couldn't find him. He was gone."

"Fuck," Kevin said.

Pud rubbed the tears from his face. He snuffled up the snot. He sensed more space around himself. He opened his eyes. They had all stepped back, but they still circled him.

"Fuck," Kevin said.

"Where were you when you last saw him?" Kyle said.

Pud scrunched his eyes shut. The truth would work. "Abandoned farm a couple miles west of Earl's," he said. "I … I was drunk and stoned. I'm not sure which one."

Kevin spoke over Pud's head, saying, "What do you want to do?"

"Tell the cops," Kyle said. "Go look for Tommy."

Pud opened his eyes. Kyle walked away from the circle, down the lane, towards the front of the store. The others fell in behind him, except for Matt and Kevin, who lingered. Kevin stooped and said, "If the cops find him dead, we'll come back for your ass."

Kevin turned and strode behind the others. Matt shot Pud a last glower, then trotted to catch up to Kevin.

Pud sat on the gravel while easing his legs in front of himself. He bent his knees up and tucked his head into the darkness. Fuckers would've killed him. He heaved himself upright and got going. He ignored the popping joints in his smashed toes.

Chapter Eleven

BamBamBam! The door-rattling bashes jarred Pud out of his doze. He jammed his foot on the hardwood floor. The gauze and the four layers of threadbare socks failed to protect his broken toes. The stab of pain dizzied him, hazed his sight, and forced a whimper out of him.

His dry eyes stung. He blinked up some moisture and his double-vision jibed to a single image. The dirty screen blurred the face at window. He shot the rest of the way out of his stupor. An instant headache joined his throbbing toes in the painful feedback ricocheting up and down his spine. He'd left only that shade up, he'd meant to sit here and watch for approaching vehicles, so he'd have plenty of time to hide, but he'd nodded off.

Pud didn't recognize the man's curly hair. The man's white shirt, unbuttoned at the throat, and dark suit jacket made Pud think 'cop,' even before the man held up his credentials and commanded, "FBI, open up."

Pud coughed. Those motherfuckers did it. *Narks*. And nobody would give them any shit about it either. He slitted his eyes.

The FBI agent jabbed his credentials towards the front door. He whisked himself from the window in the same direction.

Pud reached toward the paraphernalia scattered over the end table on his right. Between the dregs of Tommy's roach and the resin scrapings from his various pipes and one hitters, he'd managed a decent enough buzz to kill the pain. *Too decent*. He placed his tar-stained Allen wrench and straightened paper clip into the old check box, next to a pack of rolling papers and his collection of roach clips. He picked up his marble pipe. The FBI man had to have seen it all. He placed the pipe back on the table. Anyways, they wouldn't give a shit about his drug stuff. They were here to arrest him for murder.

The cool shadows of the living room taunted him. He should've stationed himself in the dark, not here between the dining room and the sun room, in broad fucking daylight. He stared at his piss-poor bandaging of his foot. He exhaled a long, hot sigh. He couldn't run if he had to. Might as well get it over with.

A single woody bash startled him. Rising, he moaned. He limped toward the front door. His trudge shook the floorboards. The door seemed a million miles away. He imagined cops standing around Tommy's grave, the black dirt piled high along one edge of the hole. He imagined them, outside the house, cruisers parked every which way, cherries flashing red, one of the cops waiting to slap a pair of shiny steel handcuffs on him.

He clasped the doorknob. He closed his eyes. He inhaled through his nose, exhaled out his mouth, a slight cough marring his calming breath. *Deserve this. Maybe.* A hacking fit savaged his throat. Moisture seeped through the seal of his eyelids. *No. They started it.*

He opened the door. Two men, one sedan. No roadblock of cruisers, no squad of cops to arrest a murderer. The curly-haired agent stood behind and one step lower than another agent, whose eyes and mouth matched the flatness of his dark buzzcut. Buzzcut's uptight posture and tie made Curls' pose seem almost casual and cool. Buzzcut reminded Pud of the Army recruiter who visited the high school during senior year, the recruiter

doing about a million pushups while trying to sucker dudes into signing up. *Pricks.*
"You're here about Tommy," Pud said.

"John Everson?" Buzzcut said.

Pud nodded.

"I'm Agent Anderson," Buzzcut said. "This is Agent Lynch. Mind if we come inside?"

"Do you have a warrant?" Pud hated how scared his voice sounded.

Curls sniffed. He said to Buzzcut, "You smell that that?"

"Smells like probable cause," Buzzcut said.

"You can be civil," Curls said, "and invite us in, or, we can cuff you, radio the locals, and let them arrest you for possession. They'll do it just to impress us."

Pud felt the slack of his jaw. He shut his mouth.

"Relax," Buzzcut said. "We're not here to bust some hayseed for a few flakes of pot."

"Fine," Pud said. "Come on in." Pud hobbled over to the kitchen table, meaning to draw them away from his mess of paraphernalia and the stronger weed stink. Out of the corner of his eye he watched them nosing about, getting a good fucking look at every little thing. He pulled out a chair and fixed its back against wall. He plopped down. He stretched out his bad foot. He fingered the edge of the square glass ashtray. He jonesed for a lady cigarettes, but they sat way over on the coffee table in the middle of his pipes and cleaning tools.

Buzzcut, his back to Pud, said, "What did you do to your foot?"

"Broke some toes," Pud said.

"Get into a fight?" Curls said.

"No." Pud scrambled for an explanation. "I dropped a dumbbell on my foot." *Stupid.* He didn't have any weights, if they cared to look. He felt the both of them sizing up his arms and coming to the conclusion that he'd never worked out a day in his life. He organized a few lies around the problem, but he should've known better. He had to be smarter.

"Where's your family?" Buzzcut said.

Pud dropped his shoulders. "Out of town for a couple weeks. I got the place to myself."

"Lucky you," Curls said. "I'd be partying down, at your age."

Pud shrugged. *Good. Loosey-goosey.*

Buzzcut circled away from the living room towards Pud. He said, "When's the last time you saw Tom Carter?"

Pud strained to remain still. His nonchalant tone pleased him as he said, "Earl's party. Couple nights ago."

"Everybody we talked to said you were the last one anybody saw with him," Curls said.

Pud dipped his chin. So they'd already talked to Kevin and the rest of the assholes. Maybe others too. He had to stick to the truth, for a while, anyways. He cocked his head, shot them a crooked smile, and said, "I was pretty drunk. Everybody was." He let his smile wither. "Including Tommy."

"*Where*," Curls said, "was the last place you saw Tommy?"

"Um …" Pud glanced toward his pot smoking chair.

Curls tracked his gaze. He performed a tight-lipped smile. "Relax," he said. "So you guys went somewhere to smoke up. Shit's scarce, didn't want to have to share with the whole damned party. I get it. We don't care about a couple of dudes sharing a joint. What we do care about is *where*."

Pud cleared his throat. "Yeah," he said. "We smoked pot." He straightened up. "I was already pretty drunk. Tommy wanted to go walking around for old time's sake." Pud looked at Curls and said, "Man, I was pretty wasted, and we just kept walking. I couldn't find that old farm we ended up at if I tried. Then once we were there, we got super baked. Honestly, I don't even remember how I got home. All I know is the place has to be … I don't know, two or three miles from Earl's."

"And that's the last time you saw Tom Carter?" Buzzcut said.

Pud wiped his forehead. *It's okay.* The pricks were 'sweating' him, after all. He wiped his hand on his shirt. "Yeah, I think so," he said. "I mean, he could've walked me home, I just can't remember." He eyeballed Curls. "He had some primo weed, and … and I shouldn't smoke after I drink. I get really messed up."

Curls nodded. Pud shifted his eyes to Buzzcut, who'd already started towards the front door. His stride seemed to draw Curls behind him. Pud leaned that way too. He caught the look the two pricks exchanged. *Burnout. Dead end.* Pud worked to keep his eyelids at a sleepy cast. As soon as they were gone, he would get rid of that damned gun. Squint couldn't nark-

Buzzcut veered toward a window. He yanked the string. The shade rolled up. He placed his hands on his hips. He pondered the countryside. "A pair of witnesses claim they saw the two of you arguing," he said.

Pud blinked. He caught Curls staring at him. He faked a few more blinks while relaxing the muscles in his face. *Pretty fucking sneaky.* Wouldn't work again, though. He didn't have to guess who those witnesses must be, Los Bastardos lying their asses off just to fuck him over. His shrug felt a bit stiff. "I don't remember arguing."

Buzzcut pivoted towards him while Curls turned away, the two of them exchanging another glance during their little move. Pud suppressed a smile. "Another witness claims you had a hassle with Tommy," Curls said.

Another witness. Squint. None of this would be happening if not for Squint. *None of it.* "I think I know who said that," Pud said. "He's the one who had a real hassle with Tommy."

Curls lowered his voice while saying, "Witnesses will testify about your old beef."

Pud found himself tilting forward in his seat and tensed all over. Both feds stared at him, drinking it all in. His broken toes throbbed. He sat back against the wall. He dropped his eyes toward his foot and said, "Ouch," He sucked in a slow breath. He had to stay cool. He couldn't fuck up now.

"You might think you're the only one in whole wide world," Curls said. "But this kind of thing happens all the time."

"Boys will be boys," Buzzcut said.

"*That* never bothered me," Pud said. He scraped his upper and lower molars sideways against each other. The scrape sounded like thunder inside his skull. Pud wanted to swallow so bad. *They know. They fucking know.*

"Don't leave town," Buzzcut said.

Pud didn't budge until their tires crunched gravel. And for a while after.

Chapter Twelve

"*Ffffaggot.*"

Pud dropped his gallon jug of water. The jug *sproinged* to a rest on the grass. Pud fumbled the brown paper bag but he managed to get his freed hand around the sack without spilling his pillow, blanket, or cigarettes. He peered towards the source of that accusation. The shadows had thickened in this last hour of daylight, darkening the dense stand of trees that marked the fenceline between the backyard and the fields beyond.

A dude rustled out of the gloom. Pud took a backwards step, spearing his broken toes against the ground. He winced. Another dude followed the first dude. And another, and more. *Kevin.* And the rest, coming to finish what they started. But before the first dude stepped into the pale shadows Pud smelled his mistake.

Their stunted scrawniness marked the pack of Muellers before the dying sunlight revealed their thinning blondish bowl-cuts, their grubby tans, and their pit-stained hand-me-down tee shirts. Their faded blue jeans flopped at their ragged hems. Pud knew a few faces, put he couldn't put a name to any of them. *Too young.* A couple couldn't be old enough yet to quit school.

"Where ya goin', fag?"

The big mouth didn't come up to Pud's chin. Hell, the dirty fucker ranked on the smallish end of the bunch, but he acted like a hardass, leading the way by a good couple of strides. The 'hardass' rocked his right side inward every other step, really playing up tough-guy pose. His sneer twisted extra-ugly at the left corner of his lips. "What's the matter," he said, "mouth too tired from sucking cocks?"

Pud bared his clenched teeth. The others snickered. Pud spat, "I nev-"

The hardass rammed Pud. The wind whooshed out of Pud's lungs. Pud dropped the bag. He doubled over. He staggered backwards. He tore himself out of the hardass's grasp. His wheezes hit a wall that stopped him from taking a decent breath. Lack of oxygen and the jagged bolts of pain from his aggravated toes woozied him.

Pud shambled toward the house. The open windows slowed him. Even if he beat them to the front door, and locked it behind himself, all they had to do was bust in through the window screens. *The gun.* If he could get to the gun, he could scare them off.

The hardass shoved Pud away from the house. Pud's feet tangled underneath himself. His elbow slammed into the grass. The jolt forced a yip out of him. The hardass shouted, "Homo!" and punted Pud's shoulder.

The hardass cranked up for another kick. He swung his foot at Pud, who shifted and snatched the hardass's ankle. The hardass screamed, "Get your fag hands off me!" Pud gritted his teeth against the pain, which intensified while he rolled himself into a sitting position. He held his attacker's ankle and rose to his feet. The hardass hopped to keep his balance. Pud secured both hands on the little fucker's ankle and lifted. The hardass yelped. Pud heaved his hands upward and released the fucker's ankle. The hardass's other leg shot off the ground. His sudden high-kick flung his sneaker off his foot and flipped the dirty shoe end over end towards the trees. His back whammed against the grass. His legs folded over his torso and rebounded back onto the ground. His busted lip oozed red.

Pud loomed over the hardass. Pud flexed his fists. The hardass dug his heels and elbows into the grass and scrabbled back from Pud. The other Muellers drew together in a clump. Pud huffed out some hot air. He loosened his fists. He fixed his best stone-cold glare on the hardass. He turned his attention to his camping gear. His pillow had popped halfway out of the brown bag onto the grass.

"Fucking faggot."

A belt buckle clinked. Pud froze. The hardass had already shucked his shirt, his other shoe, and both socks. His farmer's tan exposed splotches of red acne blighting the fish-belly white of his chest and wrinkly paunch. He unzipped his jeans.

Pud frowned. He almost said, 'And you call me a fag,' but as the kid wriggled out his jeans, revealing a thatch of blonde pubes that pretty much buried his tiny dick, Pud got it.

Pud spun. He remembered his broken toes right before he would have stomped them onto the ground. He took a few stutter steps. Behind him, a guttural groan provoked whoops from the Muellers. A wave of rancid BO overtook Pud. His eyes watered. His stomach curdled. He hobbled as fast as he could around the corner of the house.

A hard mass bashed into Pud's kidneys. A sideways whiplash wracked his spine. He corkscrewed down to one knee. Pain exploded up from his injured toes. He screamed. The hard mass crashed into his shoulder blades. The blow drove him towards the ground. He managed to get his hands underneath himself in time to save his nose from stabbing into the dirt. That awful stink clung to him, invaded his nostrils, forced his stomach to contract. He half-drooled, half-vomited a mouthful of bitter saliva onto the ground.

The squirrel slewed in a semicircle, its claws shearing up blades of grass. Clumps of blonde fur hedged the pale bald spots that blotched its pelt. It reared up on its hindquarters, bared its orangish teeth, and ejaculated a spittly hiss. Nicks and gouges flecked its yellowish claws, but the crooked nails hooked down to nasty tips. A Mueller behind Pud hollered, "Kill the cocksucker!" Another Mueller said, "Rip his fucking dick off!"

Pud pressed his torso up off the ground. He gritted his teeth. He looked behind himself. Two Muellers had already stripped off their clothes. All of their vicious little eyes glinted. One of the clothed fuckers *snicked* open a switchblade. Another cracked his knuckles, another slapped his fist against his palm. They closed in. Pud unclenched his jaw as much as the excruciating pulses from his broken toes would allow. He closed his eyes and lowered his torso to the grass. He exhaled.

"Jake!"

Pud raised his head. The freakish squirrel had dropped to all fours. Pud tracked the bearing of its greasy black eye. A different pack of Muellers rushed along the lane towards the ambush. Pud groaned. He writhed for a position of relief between his smashed toes and wrenched spine and shoulders.

A butt-ugly dude led the pack of older Muellers. "Jake!" he said. "Change back right the fuck now!" A gash split the left side of the leader's upper lip into uneven segments. A mushiness dampened the edges of his words as he said, "The rest of you get your fucking clothes on. It's fucking broad daylight for christsakes!"

The leader stopped. He planted his hands on his hips. His darkish blonde hair fringed his sunburned skull. His stooges fanned out, some towards the younger ones, the others hemming in Pud. The older Muellers' hand-me-down tee shirts and jeans showed just as many stains and holes as the younger Muellers' frayed duds. The older ones also had that same kind of tan, where Pud couldn't even understand how the sun penetrated the top layers of unwashed filth. Pud had heard the stories, he had heard some names, but he couldn't put a single name to a face. He'd had no idea that so many of the grimy fuckers were running around.

A crackling raised Pud's hackles. Reeking body-odor gagged him. By the time he blinked his watery eyes clear, the naked hardass, *Jake*, caught a pair of jeans flung at him. Sweat slicked Jake's acne-riddled chest.

The hairlip pointed at Pud while glaring at Jake. He said, "You can't kill this motherfucker."

Jake riffled his jeans up his legs. Pud darted his eyes away from Jake's glistening pubes. "Why the fuck not?" Jake said. "You know what he did."

"Yeah," the hairlip said. "I do. He put the fucking FBI on Squint."

Pud grimaced. All the Muellers, cussing and glaring, moved in on Pud. He coiled up onto his knees. They had him surrounded.

"You kill him," the hairlip said, "and the pigs will think Squint did it. And you know what'll happen if they come snooping around us. And if they throw Squint in jail, when he's this close … I don't have to tell you what that means."

Pud folded himself over his knees and into a sitting position. He stretched out his leg to relieve the pressure on his fucked-up toes.

"Fuck you," one of the younger ones said. "All we gotta do is keep Squint hid for a while."

Some of the older freaks seemed to agree with the younger ones. A heaviness dragged downward on Pud's eyelids. A younger one shoved the chest of an older one. A couple others held the other one back from attacking the shover. Their chatter went all high-pitched and squeaky. As quick as he glanced at the corner of the house, somebody warned, "You just sit your ass right there, if you know what's good for you."

The hairlip shouted, "Listen!" The others quieted, and the hairlip lowered his voice, saying, "I'd love nothing more than to dish out a little hurt to this fucking nark …"

Pud's cheeks blazed.

"… but," the hairlip said, "the fucker actually did it. You hear me? The fucker actually did it."

Pud felt their stares. His face reached a feverish temperature. He *was* a murderer. It would only take one of them going to the FBI. He raked the sweat from his forehead, dipping his hand a little to wipe away the welling teardrops.

He lowered his head. He zoned on the grass until the blades muddled into unbroken green. He tuned out their argument. He could tell them that Squint was the only witness. If Squint changed before the trial, hell, even during the trial, the case against him would fall apart. He only had to stay cool in the face of all the heat that would come his way. And when that lone witness disappeared, the cops would come snooping around the Muellers looking for him, and they would be up shit creek just the same.

He raised his eyes. Muellers shot him dirty looks. He returned to grass-gazing. If the freaks didn't figure that shit out, he would have to figure out a way to explain it to them. He could see only one way out for them. If he confessed, there'd be no need for witnesses, no need to drag Squint into this mess, no reason for the cops to snoop around the Muellers. *Fuck.* And it was the right thing to do.

He cleared his throat. He rubbed his chin while figuring out how he was gonna say it. One of them curled his hand in front of his crotch and jackhammered the thumb-side of his fist at Pud. Pud twitched. Everybody would ... he bit down on his tongue. None of this was his fault.

The hairlip looked at Pud and said, "You got something to say?"

Yeah, 'Fuck you!'

Pud shook his head. He resumed his study of the grass between his legs. He needed to get these losers out of here. If anybody saw them ...

"There's gotta be a way out of this shit," the hairlip said. "Anybody got any bright ideas?"

Pud sat back on his ass. He had to hope that one of these morons didn't stumble onto the only solution.

Chapter Thirteen

"Wallbanger! Wallbanger! Wallbanger!"

Pud puffed his cheeks and rippled the hot air out through his compressed lips. *Idiots*. Pud flexed his fingers. He inched from the darkened dining room towards the living room. The Mueller about to do the wallbanger took deep breaths, inducing a headrush. The other one on the couch kept up the chant. The other two, in chairs on the other side of the cluttered coffee table, rejoined the chant. Pud ground his teeth. Aaron, the hairlip, had said there was only gonna be two, to keep an eye on Pud while they figured out what to do. Two dirtbags had stayed, another two had turned up, and the fuckers had preceded to pound beers and smoke their stinkweed.

The hyperventilating Mueller snatched the ceramic Viking-ship bong and lit up. The bong water burbled, and burbled, and burbled. The fucker tipped his groaty face back, away from the bong's dragonhead mouthpiece. The Mueller next to him plucked the bong out of his hand. Wisps of smoke escaped from his nostrils. He sprang to his feet. He murmured, "Whoa …" He toppled over the coffee table.

The fucker's arms draped over one edge of the coffee table, his sneakers teetered off the carpet on the other side. His faded black Kiss shirt rode up and revealed a sparse tuft of long blonde hair at the small of his pale back.

One of the Muellers grunted up from his seat and heaved the wallbanger toward the couch. The wallbanger's fingers had locked onto the edge of the coffee table. He flipped the table onto its side. He bounced onto the couch. Beer cans, full ashtrays, and all the food they'd gotten into, including Pud's favorite, the cheezits and the bacon dip, spilled onto the carpet.

Pud glared at the beer soaking through the ash and butts into the carpet. He glared at the ruined crackers and dip, which he'd been saving, exerting all his will not to tear into the second he'd had the house to himself. Bongwater puddled out of the capsized Viking ship.

The three fuckers howled at the groggy fucker. One on the other side of the coffee table poured beer on the carpet, and the other fuckers laughed. The fucker next to him threw his cigarette on the carpet and ground out the coal with his heel. And the fuckers laughed. The fucker beside the wallbanger picked up the box of crackers, upended the bag, and tap-danced his sneakers on the pile of chips until he mashed them to crumbs. And the motherfuckers *laughed*.

"Foodeaters!"

The Muellers gawked at Pud. *Plip. Plip. Plip.* Pud's eyes lasered in at the nerve-grating spatter. The fucker who'd poured his beer on the carpet goggled at Pud. The fucker didn't move a muscle, his fucking arm extended. His upside-down can dripped its dregs onto the mess.

Pud drew his fists up to his hips. The fucker next to the groggy motherfucker whisked the coffee table back into its place. Another fucker joined the first in scooping mounds of butts, ash, and cracker crumbs into the square glass ashtrays and resettling the heaping trays on the coffee table. The third fucker, the one who'd dumped beer on the carpet, helped the others to gather up the empties. While lurching up from the carpet he elbowed the jumble of aluminum cans, bowling most of them back onto the floor. Cussing under his breath, he hustled to pick up empties.

Behind Pud, the front door *whinged* all the way around and banged against the wall. Pud's neck muscles stiffened. He twisted. A plague of Muellers swarmed into the house. Pud recoiled into the dark nook beside the post that separated the dining room from the living room. One dirtbag hugged a white styrofoam cooler to his scrawny chest. Another toted a bigass boombox on his shoulder, which he lowered onto an end table. The dirtbag rooted around for a wall socket. Others schlepped cardboard trays of Vartz. Pud lost count after the sixth case of the cheapass beer. A couple of rockers, stringy hair and soiled bandanas around their necks, strolled in with their arms around girls. Pud doubted that the girl who looked oldest had reached fifteen. The girls' stunted scrawniness and their dark blonde frizz suggested one of the worst rumors about the Muellers. Thrash metal erupted from the boombox. Among the cheering and howling Muellers, Pud recognized a few evil smirks of those who'd backed baldass Jake.

Pud hugged the wall all the way around the dining room, through the sunroom, and into the kitchen. Nobody noticed him. He ducked below counter-level in case anybody lurking outside might spot his escape by the weak glow of the stove light. He eased the door to the laundry room shut behind himself. In total darkness, he pressed his back against the door and listened for pursuers. His heartbeat thudded.

Pud felt his way along the washer and dryer to the door to the garage. Enough moonlight passed through the windows to light Pud's path through the debris littering the cement floor. He slipped outside. He sneaked over to the first of the sheds. He whipped himself around the open end of the shed. He took a second to breathe, now that they couldn't see him from the house.

He pulled his lady cigarettes out of the back pocket of his jeans. He situated the pack on a horizontal beam. He set his Bic next to the cigarettes on the narrow wooden shelf. From the depths of his front pocket, he fished out his marble pipe. He settled the finger-long pipe on the beam. He picked up the cigarettes and eyeballed the pack. The roach strained against the cellophane. They'd stubbed it out a few hits away from needing a clip. He figured he could squeeze two buzzes out of the nub. As he loaded the roach into his pipe's bowl, he muttered, "At least the scuzzballs are good for something."

He lit up. The taste of burnt tar invaded his mouth. He hung in there until he'd filled his lungs. He thumbed the bowl in order to snuff out the smoldering roach. He held his breath as long as he could. A ragged wheeze ended his exhale, but he managed not to cough.

His second hit ripped him up. He hacked. He peeked around the wall at the house. He guessed nobody could hear a fucking thing over the noisyass metal. The Muellers had parked three beaters along the lane. He found it hard to believe that all those freakasses fit into those three shitboxes. He knew they were scarfing all his food, fucking up the place, and probably stealing stuff. He couldn't stand to watch their headbanging silhouettes anymore. He stepped behind the shed wall and smoked another, more modest hit.

He closed his eyes. Things shifted. He sighed. He sagged against the wall. They were doing it on purpose. To get back at him. They couldn't kill him, and they couldn't beat him up, because that would make Squint look guiltier.

He sparked a cigarette. The first drag lifted him a little higher. *Squint*. This had to be all Squint's idea. Fucker wanted revenge, but couldn't say shit. The only way Squint could get back at him was to trash his house.

He took another drag. *Fucking Squint*. Devious little motherfucker. Squint blabbing to all his kin was another way Squint had fucked him over. One of them was bound to open his big mouth, and Squint could always say, 'Hey, I didn't rat you out, even after you narked on me.' Maybe Squint was so close to changing forever that he didn't give a fuck what anybody thought. Hell, the little fucker might've already changed over for good.

He drew on his cigarette until his throat burned. His coughs doubled him over. He slid down the wall and sat on the dirty concrete. *Fuck*. He might as well save himself the trouble and turn himself in. He rubbed his dry eyes. He'd murdered another human being in cold blood. He deserved to go to prison.

He tilted his head back against the wall. He closed his eyes. He would call the FBI first thing tomorrow morning. Buzzcut would give a monotone reading of his rights while the Curls cuffed him. Then gray walls, iron bars, and a cafeteria like at school except that everybody dressed the same. At least he wouldn't have to worry about his shitty clothes. He coughed up a laugh.

He clapped his free palm over his mouth. He winced. He dropped his palm and bowed his head. He took a deep drag and blew the hot smoke out of his nostrils. He whispered, "Do you really think it's funny?" Tommy had been trying to hard to apologize for what he, what they, did. Tommy had admitted that what they did had ruined his life.

He shook his head. That shit wasn't funny. He sniffled. He closed his eyes. He crinkled his forehead. He conjured that ring-around-the-rosy of mouths, teeth, sharp teeth, laughing so fucking hard, the ring orbiting while seesawing around him. His guts knotted up. *The motherfuckers*, *the rat bastards*, everything bad in his life ... and the ring of laughing teeth spun. And flickered. Another flicker. Then another.

He should have forgiven Tommy when he had the chance. The spinning teeth streaked up and away, its tracers a jagged smear that faded into total blackness. He planted his palms on the gritty concrete. He swallowed his gorge. His stomach seemed to sling back into its rightful place. He opened his eyes.

High beams strafed the weeds in front of the shed. Pud groaned. *More Muellers*. He pinched the butt of his dropped cigarette and brought it to his lips. He sucked hard and the cigarette's coal fired. His trembles stilled. The weeds brightened from dark green to a sickly yellow as the car neared. He frowned. Even over the noise metal rattling out of the house, he should've heard the car's fucked-up engine, if the newcomers drove a Mueller vehicle. *FBI*. He snorted. More likely cops, the county boys, the racket carrying all the way to the highway, coming to bust up the party. *Let them*. It'd be the best thing to happen to him since … forever.

The lights died. The weeds returned to spiky dark shapes. Pud frowned. Cops would flash their cherries, they always did.

Minding his broken toes, he rolled onto his hands and knees. He peered around the corner. The car idled in front of the house. Could be one of his mom's nosy friends. But despite the darkness, the car vibed 'new' to him, and none of his mom's friend could afford that. *Fuck*. Word must of got out that Pud was having a party. With every fucking body back in town, it could be any of his former classmates. By tomorrow morning, everybody would be talking about the crazy shit the Muellers did at Pud's party.

He scurried out to meet the car. He didn't have a fucking clue what he was gonna say to make them turn back before they saw-

All four doors swung open. Pud stopped dead in his tracks. The dome light revealed Matt's high forehead. Pud would've recognized Kyle's square build in the dark. Kevin glared at Pud from behind the wheel before levering his bumpy frame out of the car. Sour-faced Trent slouched out of the front passenger's side. They all slammed their doors good and hard.

Pud stepped backward. The assholes fell in behind Kevin, who strode towards Pud. Kevin's snarl made Pud slide back another step. The pain in his toes blasted through the numbness of his buzz. No way could he outrun the assholes, or juke around them and make a run for the house.

Kevin growled, "What happened to Tommy?"

Pud swallowed. "I don't know," he said. His pot-sludged voice came out all weak and cracked, making his claim sound like a lie.

Matt sneered, "That what you told the cops?"

FBI, you fucking nark, Pud wanted to say. He cleared his throat and said, "I told them the truth."

"So you're gonna stick to your story," Kevin said. His massive Cro-Magnon forehead shadowed his eyes in the dark, but Pud felt their jitter, the big asshole chomping at the bit to put his huge fists to work. "Tommy asked you to forgive him and you said 'fuck you' and ran away."

Pud mashed his lips together. He couldn't remember exactly what he told them the last time they'd pushed him around. He couldn't get his brains chugging.

A *thwack* at his ear surprised a yip out of him. He jumped away. His earlobe throbbed. The pain felt wet. Matt's familiar snicker followed. The fuckhead had snuck up behind him and flicked him on the earlobe, right on the scab from the last time. The fuckhead never missed.

Matt dodged back into the pack. "Answer him," he said. "Cocksucker."

Pud cradled his ear. The blood wetted his palm. "I told you the truth," he said.

"You're lying," Trent said. Pud glanced over his right shoulder. Trent had floated to the side, trying to sneak behind him too. "One thing about good ol' Puddy," Trent said, "always ready with a lie to save his own ass."

Pud flinched. His tone rose near to a whine as he said, "Nobody says that about me."

Kevin grabbed Pud by the shoulders. He shoved Pud backwards. Pud fell flat on his ass. Kevin loomed over Pud and said, "Squint said that Tommy never talked to him."

"Why didn't he talk to Squint," Matt said, "like he said he was gonna?"

Pud floundered. The fall had knocked the wind out of him, and he couldn't get enough air in to think.

"Tommy wouldn't have just given up," Kyle said. "That wasn't his style."

They stared at Pud. Machinegun riffs blazed from the house.

Kyle glanced over his shoulder at the rowdy house. He nodded the other way and said to the others, "Let's take him back there."

They dragged him back behind the shed. Knuckles burrowed into his kidneys. The sharp agony cut off his scream before it got halfway up his throat. Just like back then. He'd dug his heels into the gravel but they were too strong, so he gave up, and went limp while they hauled him all the way back into the locker room showers. Where Trent and Kyle stood guard over Squint.

They pinned him against the shed's wall. Trent stood guard at the corner of the shed. Matt said, in a sing-song lilt, "Watch out, he might get a boner."

Pud roared, "No!" He blasted into them. He knocked Kevin down. Matt pinwheeled his arms before he lost his balance and hit the dirt. Pud's surge even forced Kyle to back-peddle a few steps. Pud jabbed his index finger toward Kevin and spat, "This is all *your* fault!"

They all froze. Fuckhead Kevin and fuckhead Matt stayed on their asses. He puffed up his chest. If he had knocked them down before ... "Tommy would ..." He chomped his mouth shut.

Kevin stirred.

"*Would*," Kyle said, "what?"

Pud's attention darted to Kyle. On his periphery, the others rose, and boxed him in. "He would ..." he said. "He would ..."

"Fuck, what the fuck?"

Pud looked beyond that assholes towards the pair of Muellers staggering towards them. The assholes seemed twice as big as they turned to face down the sloshed runts. Another Mueller sidled around the corner of the shed.

"Go back to your party," Kyle said. "This is none of your business."

"Oh," said another, more sober-sounding Mueller, this one rounding the other side of the shed, with another pair behind him, "but it is. See, Pudsly here is our pal."

More Muellers, three, then two behind them, then more, and Pud lost count, emerged from the weeds on the other side of the railroad tracks. A few Muellers stood as tall as Kyle, but they all looked like stick figures in comparison. Sharp stick figures with absolutely nothing good to lose.

Kyle leveled dead eyes at Pud. Kyle turned his back on Pud. Kyle stalked toward the Muellers, who withdrew at least punching distance away from him. The other assholes followed. Matt sniffed at Pud on his way out. Matt grimaced.

A random Mueller laughed. He hollered, "Let's get this party started!" The Muellers whooped it up. The mob streamed towards the house.

Pud backed up to the shed's wall. He slewed down to the dirty concrete. He glanced up at his pack of lady cigarettes, which still sat on that frame beam. *Too far*. He pulled his legs up and wrapped his arms around them. He rested his forehead on his kneecaps. He'd almost told.

Chapter Fourteen

Screech.

Pud snuffled awake while hinging his torso off the dirty rug. He lunged to catch the spider plant ... daylight lanced through his skull. Dust stung his dry eyeballs. He shut his eyelids. *Screech.* The noise, from somewhere below, honed his headache. He slumped. He inhaled a whiff of old mouse turds and stale poison. He coughed. The spider-plant incident had happened last night. Just one of the many 'accidents.' Finally, he could't take it anymore and he'd climbed into the attic and locked the hatch door behind himself.

He moaned. He cracked his eyelids. Motes swirled in the sunlight shafting through the smudged window. He had tried to open that window last night, but it wouldn't budge. He coughed. The stuffy heat exhausted his lungs.

Screech. He winced. He mumbled, "What the fuck are they doing now?" He levered himself up to his feet, minding his broken toes, which pounded a distant beat. The effort of rising provoked a sweat. He swiped his forearm across his gritty brow. He had to get the fuck out of here. He opened the hatch and backed down the steps, which joinged under his weight.

Screech!

His headache cranked up a notch. Snoring drew him to his mother's bedroom door. He shook his head. He couldn't understand how anybody could sleep through that piercing noise. He nosed up to his mother's ajar bedroom door. On top of the torn up bedding, the naked body of a bony girl sprawled over a naked Mueller. The girl's dirty blonde hair, pimply pale skin, and ribby figure duplicated the Mueller's. They could've been twins. *Fuck, might be.* He shuddered. He looked to the floor, his gaze landing on a bunched up pair of tighty-whities, and the brown skidmark streaking the yellowed fabric. He jettisoned the room's air out of his nostrils. He backed into the hallway. He sagged against the wall. They had infested all the bedrooms. He had to wash all the bedding, and hope to fucking God that the ... *juices* ... didn't seep through and stain the mattresses, the funk puffing out of the fabric forever.

Screech!

He jerked away from the wall. His broken toes bumped the floorboards. He closed his eyes and waited out the agony. He limped to the stairwell. Halfway down, another, louder screech tightened his headache, so that his skull seemed to constrict.

At the bottom of the stairs, direct sunlight forced him to shield his eyes. The front door offered an escape from this waking nightmare, but he had to see for himself. He veered towards the kitchen, towards the source of that earsplitting screech.

The baseboard of the cabinet between the fridge and the stove dammed one side of a puddle. Some asswad had tossed a kitchen towel half in the rounded side of the puddle. Yellow had soaked into the towel up to the last inches on the dry linoleum. Just past the towel, a curled pile of dog turds dashed his hopes that some dickwad had spilled beer.

A mess of overturned bottles and beer cans littered the countertops and the stovetop, the odd bottle or crumpled can having tumbled to the floor. Upended cracker and cereal boxes proved that the vermin had raided the pantry.

SCREECH!

He staggered backwards. He cupped his palms over his ears. The shriek threatened to shatter his skull. A bleary gray bird perched on the faucet. Yellow-fringed white ooze splotched the stainless steel perch. Pud's hip banged a chair onto its back. The razor bursts of pain from his toes did not slow his scurry to the front door. He opened the door.

Slabs of furry brown muscle clipped the back of his kneecap. The door's frame bashed his shoulder. The brown blurs banged open the screen door. His bad foot stomped onto the cement riser outside. The screen door rattled against his other shoulder. The blurs resolved into two pitbulls, right before they hurtled into the weeds. He belched. A little acid soured the end of that belch. He didn't want to know what freakyass squirrel shit they might have done after he'd hid in the attic last night.

He shut the door behind himself. He limped out from under the awning. The sun reduced his vision to red strips. From his temples to his chin, sweat carved runnels through the crust of dehydrated sweat and attic dust. A distant *screech* killed his smile.

Through the greasy window of a Mueller shitbox, he spotted a keychain hanging from the ignition switch. He got in behind the wheel. His backside settled into the hot black plastic seat cover. His eyelids drooped. His head's swaying nod snapped to attention. He scrunched his eyes. He could park in the shade alongside some lonely gravel road and get some fucking sleep.

He started up the piece of shit. The gas needle jumped to F. It was gonna be a motherfucking bitch to clean the house. He rested his head against the steering wheel. *Didn't matter*. No matter how hard he worked, he would miss something, probably a lot of things. For sure his mother would find out. The wobbles of the mistimed pistoned agitated through his brow and rippled to his slack lips. Everybody would find out.

Nobody would think he was all buddy-buddy with the Muellers if they'd seen those motherfuckers flick burning cigarettes at his hair. He resettled himself against the seat cushion. The headrest nestled the back of his skull. He tapped his fist against the steering wheel. Scorched ends bristled his fingertips around the patch where his hair had caught fire. They had laughed their asses off. They had called him names, one motherfucker calling him *Pud G-*

His fist chopped against the steering wheel. His yip quavered along with another faint screech. He cradled the heel of his palm. He'd had to stand there and take it. They had all made sure that he knew *they knew*. Kept calling him *Killer*, and *Psycho*. One of the fuckers would nark, no doubt. Squint maybe already had.

A wiggle haunted a molar. Unclamping his teeth forced a grunt out of him. The gas needle hovered at F. Maybe get the fuck out of Dodge. Another fucking screech sounded from the house. He would have to go into hiding. A federal fugitive, he might as well become a riverbilly.

Tommy had the right idea. *Admit you fucked up, admit you deserve punishment*.

Percolating gravel cut off his sniffle. The FBI sedan cruised toward the house. He cut the engine and got out of the car.

The sedan slowed, swooped, stopped. Their park-job blocked the lane. Like he was gonna hop in the car and make a break for it. *Pricks*. Curls rocked himself out of the passenger side. Buzzcut marched around the front of the sedan. Buzzcut snooped towards the house, while buttoning his suit coat.

The breeze whisked Curls blonde locks behind his shoulders. He chomped on gum. "Blowing town?"

Pud snorted. Buzzcut weaved through the Mueller junkers while stealing looks at the house. Curls' approach slowed to a stalk. *Motherfucking pricks.*

A muted screech wrenched the agents' scrutiny to the house. Their stares strobed through each other, then fixed upon Pud. Buzzcut said, "He's probably going to meet up with his circle-jerk buddies."

Pud parted his lips. He shut his mouth. *No.* These pricks weren't worth it.

They crowded in on either side of Pud. "We came around," Curls said, "to see if you wanted to pitch in with the search today."

"All your circle-jerk buddies are going to be there," Buzzcut said.

A tic fussed the corner of Pud's mouth. He inhaled through his nostrils, filling his chest to capacity. Pricks came around to fuck with him, and that was fucking all there was to it.

"Today," Buzzcut said, "we ought to find that abandoned farmhouse where you claim to have last seen last Tom Carter."

The shitbox's door grazed Pud's ass. He angled his hip into the scummy metal, trying to pass his backward shuffle off as a casual lean. Each fidget seemed to nudge him deeper into a guilty awkwardness. Kyle and the rest of those assholes were sure to blab to the agents all about what he said last night. *So what?* It was pretty fucking obvious that these pricks had already decided that he did it.

Another muffled screech lured the agents' interest. Curls kept his eyes on the house while saying, "We're expecting specially trained dogs today. Dogs that can smell corpses."

The breeze ruffled Pud's hair. He couldn't help picturing a pack of Dobermans going nuts over that mound of stony dirt.

"You really got to see these dogs in action," Buzzcut said. "We can give you a ride, if you want."

"Um …" Pud said. Sweat trickled down his ribs. He'd opened his big fat mouth before he'd figured out what he was gonna say.

"He did it *osssiffferrr.*"

The Mueller's frizzy head poked out from the crack behind the ajar screen-door. The rotten gap in place of his front teeth deranged the Mueller's shit-eating grin. That sewer mouth had run nonstop all last night, shit-talking, guffawing, sometimes exhaling putrid fumes right into Pud's face.

Acids raged against the lining of Pud's stomach. Contracting, he braced himself for the shitmouth to start narking.

"He did it all right," Curls said.

Pud tensed his throat. His swallow doubled back his tongue. His gag reflex boomed in his own ears.

"Did you see him do it?" Buzzcut said.

The Mueller's bare feet slapped a swaggering groove against the concrete steps and the walkway. Each footfall jiggled his pale paunch over the waistband of his frayed jean shorts. A slight whistle infected his fake twang while he said, "I saw him I did." His festering grin widened, his eyelids stretched into black crescents. "I saw him. I saw him try to suck his own cock. Almost broke his golldarned neck."

Buzzcut glowered. One side of Curls' mouth smiled. Pud let off a stream of hot gas though his lips. His stomach calmed.

"What's your name, son?" Buzzcut asked.

The Mueller's smile vanished. His eyes narrowed to flat slits. "Ain't your son," he said. "Name's Nunya. As in, 'None ya fuckin' business,' 'less you got a warrant."

Pud stared at the dirty Mueller. *Shut up shut up shut up*!

The Mueller crowed, "I know my rights, *osssiffffersssss*!"

Curls smirked.

"We don't have time for this," Buzzcut said. He marched to the sedan.

Curls said to Pud, "You coming?"

Pud's attempt to seem breezy sounded desperate to himself as he said, "I got a house full of these jokers. Maybe I'll catch up with you later."

"Suit yourself," Curls said.

The stooped Mueller strutted up beside Pud, who tried not to recoil from the dude's noxious BO. They watched the sedan drive off. The Mueller said, "Make sure you tell everybody how I stood up to those pigs."

Pud nodded. He wasn't gonna tell anybody a goddamned thing.

Screech.

"Motherfucker," the Mueller said. He went to one of the shitboxes. He fished out a tiny birdcage and a big black towel. As he passed Pud on the way back to the house, he said, "You better've buried that body deep, mothafucka."

Chapter Fifteen

The giggle neared. Pud flattened his belly against the tough grass. He parted the yellow-green blades before his eyes. Green leaves and brown bark walled the far side of the clearing. A husky chuckle confirmed the approach of the camouflaged giggle. A few rows deep, tee-shirt white clashed with the brown and green density. He mashed the side of his fist against his lips. His fist silenced a chunky burp. The fucking horndogs were supposed to be walking straight lines with their search team, not feeling each other up in the woods.

The distance muddled her curt response, but her mewl promised that she would barely put up a fight. The dude whined for it. They wouldn't fuck in the trees. They would want a nice, soft patch of grass. In the middle of the green clearing, the twisted branches of the dead tree shaded the pile of dirt. Only a complete idiot could miss the grave. He reached for the rake lying beside him. He squeezed the wooden handle. He loosened his grip. He squeezed again.

The giggler bolted in the opposite direction. The dude crashed after her. The racket of their game of catch-me-if-you-can dwindled to stillness. Pud laid his baking forehead on the grass. His joints slackened. The urge to curl onto his side and tuck his hands under his head engulfed him. *Just give up.*

The tar sticking to the bottom of his throat outlasted his hock, which stretched into a phlegmy cough. He rasped, "Kill for a Shasta right now." He rolled onto his side. A bird's melody faded. The concept of moving a single muscle wearied him. *Shouldn't've smoked that whole roach.*

He used the rake to post himself upright. He kept his weight off his mangled toes. *Fucking space-case.* He clamped his jaw and hobbled toward the grave. He had to get this shit done before the FBI showed up.

A headrush flooded his senses. His knees wavered. He thunked the rake against the ground. The yaw of his weight slowed. He teetered on the tipping point. Gravity tractor-beamed him. He released the rake and flailed his hands. The high grass bedded his landing. Static smothered the outside world. He capsized onto his back. That roach, maybe just a toke or two below maintaining its status as a joint, he shouldn't've smoked that whole bigass roach. Those motherfuckers wasted so much goddamned pot.

Red splotches blanched the buzzing static. A deep breath fed the splotches. He took a careful, static-melting breath at each juncture on his way up to his feet. The mound's crusty brown screamed 'shallow grave' against a murder victim. Maybe rain, or maybe some fuckface Mueller had carved the dirt into that shape. The dead tree at the head of the grave might as well have been a fucking tombstone. *Fucking Squint.*

He returned to raking over the rest of the brown dirt. He locked into a rhythm. After he took care of this shit, he would go find that farmhouse and burn the place to the ground. He just had to hope that the 'borrowed' shitbox didn't break down between here and the other place. He couldn't think of anything else. Except dealing with the Mueller infestation. He grunted up a little more muscle for his next stroke. The thud of the tines against the dirt sent an aftershock along the rake that rattled his finger bones. No use cleaning anything until he got those fuckers out of the house.

A dirt clod spoiled the level ground. He swung the rake. *Fuck*. His swing softened to a prod. If anything, the wider, neater patch of black stood out more. He'd made it worse. His chin grazed his breastbone. His lips shriveled halfway into an attempt at a stoner smirk. He released the rake. The thud stimulated a remote metallic quiver from of the tines. He wasn't gonna get away with it.

He murmured, "You deserve it."

He crinkled his eyelids shut. He pressed his palm across his sockets. The ring-around-the-rosy of grins materialized. The white fangs revolved like a cartoon. *Not real*. He stopped the revolutions. He strained to recall the faces around those fangs. He couldn't erase the jagged red lines crisscrossing the whites of Tommy's eyes, and the sag of the blue-black bags under them. He couldn't forget Squint mouthing *Fuck it*. Right before. Like the little shit just wanted to get it over with. Pud scrunched his eyelids harder. The background darkened. He scrunched harder. The background blackened. As hard as he could.

He couldn't help it. Squint. Squint was the one who was into it.

Pud flicked his palm from his eyes and slapped his nuts. *Murderer*. He softened. The morning sunshine aggravated his retinas. He might as well turn himself in. If Kevin and Matt and all the assholes had figured it out, then anybody could. The Muellers knew for fuck's sure. Probably everybody else in the whole fucking town believed he did it. The FBI sure as shit thought he was guilty. Probably the whole point of their little visit this morning was to trick him into saying something stupid. Or doing something stupid. Something stupid like driving straight to the motherfucking grave the second they were out of sight. He scanned the edges of the clearing. "Nah," he said. They would've jumped out of the bushes by now.

He picked up the rake. Grass rustled. A squirrel, the freak's blonde shoulders showing above the green blades, eyeballed Pud from about halfway back to the trailhead. Pud breathed, "Jesus fucking Christ." The squirrel cocked its bullish head. Purple sores spotted the pale bald patches that afflicted its dirty blonde pelt. Its snarl bared a single orangish tooth on the left corner of its jaws … "Jake?"

The squirrel's greasy black eye didn't blink.

Pud twirled the rake into a slantwise position to guard his torso. The foremost tendrils of that burnt popcorn stink invaded his nostrils. He tried and failed to puff the stink out before the stew of swampass musk and teenage armpit saturated his tongue and everything else inside his mouth.

He hefted the business end of the rake. No way he'd get to the gun now. *Doesn't matter*. He'd held a bunch of them off, at night, with nothing but sticks and stones. He licked his lips. "Jake," he said, "I don't know if you can understand me right now, but these woods are crawling with people, and if they see you like that …"

A pair of horseflies deviled the squirrel's mangy nub of a tail.

Pud guessed he'd better take the long way back to the car. He took a backward step while keeping his eyes on the motionless squirrel. He risked a glance. To his left, a gap shanked between trunks. Clumps of itchweed narrowed the footpath, but the going would be way better than busting through the tangle of weeds, saplings, and slender branches between the other trees. Among the leaves high in the trail's first tree, a flick of a tail betrayed a squirrelish shadow. *Motherfucker. Fine*, if he had to go through Jake, then fuck it.

Three monstrosities blocked his path. One of the sneaky freaks lowered its yellow-clawed paw into the high grass, ruining the trick. They were fucking with him, just fucking with him. He refused to track the disturbances in the trees all around the clearing. He refused to give them the satisfaction. He windmilled the rake, going for a kung fu vibe, and managed to clutch the gyrating pole before it flipped out of his hands.

He steered his pitch from shrill to a warning growl while saying to the zittiest squirrel, "Go away or I'll start yelling. The searchers will see you."

A squirrel shambled out of the weeds. Its shaggy head loomed behind the front trio. Tiny squirrels sprang up around its paws and plunged back into the grass. The big squirrel plumped onto its ass. A floppy greenish hose dangled from one of its forepaws. It snagged the hose with its other forepaw. It gnawed at the section between its paws. Its gnawing agitated the long end, which hung from the squirrel's clutches. Pink gashes showed where the squirrel had chewed through the scales to the meat. At the very end, the snake's head jittered while the squirrel gouged.

Behind him, the grass swished. He dodged. The squirrel's lunge clipped his hip and spun him sideways. The squirrel blasted a straight line through the grass away from him. All around him, freakish squirrels rioted. Pud clasped the rake against his torso. Something low to the ground thrashed grass tassels toward him. Two regular squirrels burst out from cover. They tumbled over one another, right over the toes of his sneakers. One scrabbled out from the other and raced across the grave. The other darted after the first into the grass on the other side of the dirt. He exhaled a shaky breath. They were just playing, just fucking with him, because he had trespassed into their territory, into their habitat.

Cobs hammered Pud's shoulder blades. The cobs hooked the fabric of his tee shirt. Hind legs slapped against his lower back. The heft of the piggybacking squirrel swayed Pud's flinch into a stooped flail for balance. The squirrel's moist, bristly underbelly smooshed around Pud's head and neck. The boiling stink invaded his mouth and nostrils, burning his eyes. Sputtering, Pud reached over himself and grabbed fistfuls of greasy hide. He flung the squirrel over himself. The squirrel tore up gouts of black dirt while blundering over the grave. It squealed away into the grass. Pud spat. The stink clung to him. Slime streaked the back of his neck. All around him, chittering, *laughter*. Laughing their asses off. He leaned on the rake. *Roughhousing*, that's all it was.

The pimply squirrel, Jake, sprang. Pud twisted away from hissing teeth. Nails clawed the side of his neck. The gashes burned. Pud growled while sweeping the rake over his head. His roar punctuated his growl when the tines spiked into the squirrel's backside. The impact jarred the rake out of his hands. The squirrel threw its head back and screeched.

The squirrel scuttled, shrieking, the tines sunk into its flesh, the rake's pole jouncing against one flank, all the way into the trees. The hurt squirrel's passage into the dense green transfixed the others.

Pud gulped down the 'I'm sorry' poised on the tip of his tongue. He dropped his outstretched arms and squeezed his hands into fists. He ran. The pain of his mangled toes registered a blip in his skew to evade the biggest squirrel's tardy swipe. He plowed into the trees. His hands warded off whippy branches. He bounced off a few immovable boles. He ignored the trail and beelined for the car. The Bondo-red flickered through the green and brown. His momentum forced him to brace himself to a stop against the side of the grainy red metal. The key still plugged the ignition switch. He scrambled into the driver's seat. He held his breath while he turned the key. The engine fired. As he backed the shitbox up, he struggled to keep one eye on the trees and the other on the grassy ruts. The car kept slurving off the dirt grooves. Branches grazed the side panels. The rugged terrain shivered the junker, preventing Pud from gunning it. He reached a bulge in the trail wide enough to turn the car around. Once facing the right way, he jammed the shifter into Drive.

Claws scratched across the roof. He hunkered over the steering wheel. A dirty blonde blur crashed into the trees. He punched the gas pedal. The tires spun out in the grass. A thwack against the rear passenger side rocked the car. The tires caught traction. The car spurted. Thick branches and weeds swiped the passenger side, slowing down the car. A thump against his door made him flinch and left a small inward dent. Another thump against the backend of the cab spider-cracked the rear windshield. Branches buffeted the front windshield. He overcorrected, steering the car into the foliage edging the other side of the trail. He yanked the wheel the other way. A brownish mass whammed into his window. The sun dazzled through a break in the trees on the passenger side.

The car keeled over. Grass rushed at the windows. The roll flung Pud into the passenger seat, then tossed him against the roof. The car creaked onto its side, folding Pud against the driver's window. The battered car wavered on the lower edge between its side panels and its undercarriage. The car tipped, crashing onto its tires. The engine died.

Pud grabbed the wheel and craned himself up. Squirrels bombed out of the trees. A squirrel crumpled the hood. Its bulk jounced the car. It dipped its dirty blonde snout. The fractured windshield framed the spray of orangish mucus quivering on its yellowed whiskers. Hisses surrounded him. His jaw trembled. The hisses closed in, swelling to a hoarse grate that clogged every chance around him. *Dead meat*. He chomped. His trembles quieted.

The squirrels bolted.

"Hey," somebody normal yelled. "Over here!"

Pud slouched down in the seat. Soles skidded down the ditch, denim swished through grass, and a long whistle droned. Somebody said, "Fuck a duck!"

Pud shrugged their hands away after they pulled him from the wreck. He refused to lie down. He blinked until the fuzzies resolved into one coherent perspective. Raw bursts from his elbow pulsed over the distress signals of scattered scrapes and contusions. His joints crackled while he gestured at the wreck, saying, "Had a little car trouble."

Nobody really laughed. So many new sneakers, so many intact hems of pants … a striped shirt challenged Pud's focus. Somebody would give him a ride home. Where he would find the Muellers waiting for him.

"What are you doing out here?"

"What?" Pud said. He shielded his eyes. "Oh, I was trying to catch up to you guys. I guess I got lost."

Out of the flurry, a specific question hooked his attention. He said, "The trail just sort'a peters out in a field. Nothing there." He pointed in the opposite direction. "You guys been over there?"

Chapter Sixteen

"Tommy's dead." Pud sniffled. He waited to feel better. Confession was supposed to be good for the soul. He felt like puking. He wanted to lay his head on the kitchen table. The struggle to level his chin made his neck spasm, probably made him look like a weasel. The evening shadows touched the cheeseball knicknack sitting in the middle of the formica tabletop. Ceramic prayerhands bookended a row of unopened letters. Red paper showed through a few of the envelopes' little plastic windows.

Across the room, the icebox's motor ticked a beat that spiderlegged against Pud's eardrums. Pud kept his eyes hat-in-hand low. He tried to look sorry. Throbs gathered in his shattered toebones, then torched up the mashed nerves, their aftershocks chilling his foot. The burn from his skinned elbow fevered the mushy backpulses. He couldn't feel the scratches on his neck anymore. *Had a little fenderbender.* He guessed leading the searchers away from the grave all the fucklong day had ruined parts of his foot for good.

Pud gripped the seat of his wooden chair. *You goddamn pussy.* Just get it over with. Pud inhaled through his nose. He met Lyle's gray stare. "I killed Tommy," he said. He sat up straighter. He let go of his seat and clasped his hands in his lap.

Lyle ran his fingers through his salty flattop. White stubble prickled his sunburnt jaw. He didn't blink. Pud watched the ex-cop digest his confession. Lyle would know what to do. These days Lyle wore farm-faded overalls, but Pud remembered the cop's clean blue uniform and shiny black hoslter riding high on his hip back when, as landlord, he used to come around to the house he rented to Pud's mother, to fix a leak or whatever, afterwards slipping on his mirrored shades before cruising away in the town's squad car. *Should've done this in the first place.*

Lyle gnawed a thumbnail.

The icebox's random ticking was starting to drive Pud up the wall. He had to look. He lowered his candid gaze and stared off into the distance. A couple flat magnets pinned a certificate to the icebox door. Despite the cooling dusk, the fancy-shmancy gold letters dominated the certificate enough to read. *Christian Peace Officers' Benevolent Fellowship's Man of the Year.* Pud read it again, but the words jumbled to the point of nausea.

Lyle had gone on to the other thumbnail. Pud let those gold Jesus letters fuzz. He'd take his medicine like a man. And he'd take all of Squint's dirty little secrets to the grave. Fucker might have everybody else fooled, but the little piece of shit wouldn't look down his nose now, now that they couldn't get to him, now that they couldn't stop him from telling all about their freaky asses anytime he wanted.

Lyle raked his thumbnail underneath his front teeth. "I could get in a lot of trouble here," he said. He frowned at the remnants of his nail's quick. He switched to gnawing on the nail on his tobacco-browned middle finger. His frown harshed, like he was about to say 'Leave me out of it.' Pud loosened his white-knuckling hands.

"I could get cheated out of the reward," Lyle said. His pupils crossed a little bit as he went back to ratting on his nail. Gray faded the blue bags under his eyes. His cheekbones flexed and relaxed, again and again, straining his muzzle from a droop to leather and back again.

A toilet-plunger *pop* startled Pud. Lyle muttered a string of pulpy cusses while slurping his dentures around until they resocketed. Pud regarded the prayerhands knicknack.

Lyle used the ball of his thumb to give his dentures one last press against his palate. He sphinctered out his spitty thumb. "Why did you do it?"

He oughtta spill every juicy little detail. It would serve them right, serve them all right. Could set up an insanity defense. Pud kept his focus on those 'Please God Jesus' steepled fingers. No fucking help there. He guessed, starting right now, he should copy God and shut the fuck up.

Pud centered his most hardass look on Lyle, whose eyes had gone all dirty. Fucker knew damn well why, every fucking body did. Bet anything, since Tommy went missing, nobody talked about anything else. Lyle practically drooled for juicy details. He guessed he'd better get used to seeing that dirty greed from everybody. Except those motherfuckers who started it all in the first place. But they would keep their mouths shut because they knew everybody would blame them too.

Lyle leaned back in his chair. He let out a quiet snort. His eyes dried up. "First thing in the morning," he said.

"What?"

"Come back first thing in the morning." Lyle chomped his dentures a couple of times. "If we do it now, you'll just end up spending the night in a cell. First thing in the morning, I'll escort you in. In the meantime, I'll get everything set up. Lawyer, judge, let 'em know we're coming. But you gotta git ... I could be liable for harboring a fugitive."

Lyle's stare flattened. He'd made up his mind. The gentlist bend of Pud's pinky toe rumbled a warning up his nerves. A mile and a half. By the highway. He'd have to hike rougher terrain, as the crow flies. Maybe with a houseful of Muellers waiting, just hoping he'd show his face. But maybe things had gotten so hot that they didn't dare get caught dead around his place. Fuck, maybe the cops were waiting on him instead.

Lyle stood up. His back creaked straight. Pud pressed his palms against the table and eased his weight onto his feet. Pud couldn't tell if Lyle was gonna shake his hand.

Lyle swayed a touch away from Pud. "Get yourself cleaned up and wear your Sunday best," he said. "You could still get the book thrown at you if you come acting like a punk."

Pud nodded. He more than half expected it to go this way. If he had to, he could camp out till dawn, sneak in and get his shit together, and get the whole fucking thing over with before lunchtime.

Chapter Seventeen

Pud's calf cramped. The kink snapped him out of his stupor too late to keep his knee joint from bucking. His sneaker shredded rubber against the concrete. The scuff made him nip his tongue. He worried the cramp with one hand while bracing his other palm against the grimy nose of the John Deere mower. He sat up straight against the shed's backwall. He slowed his breathing down to dead silence. A breeze swished through the ditch grass.

He dug into the cramp. He peered over the riding mower's nose at the open end of the shed. He loosened the cramp to where he hoped he could run. *Fuck*. He'd been so fucking tired it hadn't even crossed his mind how he'd trapped himself between the wall and the mower. No way he'd make it past anybody at the other end, even without the cramp. The open end framed the weeds choking the ditch. Beyond the ditch the field faded into black too dense to make out the highway. There was nowhere to run.

Through the flimsy wall behind him, the house still sounded empty. The slantwise plummet of his head startled him wide awake before his chin rebounded off his breastbone. He used his fingertips to massage his cheek skin downward, maxing out the width of his eyes. If he started snoring he was dead. He had to get out. Either do it or get the fuck out of Dodge.

Fucking Lyle. The asshole had practically pushed him out the front door while scolding him to come back 'first thing in your Sunday best.' He sniffed. He couldn't smell himself anymore. Not a good sign. All he had to do was to sneak in as far as the kitchen. Garage, laundry room, kitchen. Clean clothes, food and water, and soap, even if it had to be laundry powder. He could find a spigot someplace else to wash up.

The bags under his eyes bunched up against his sinking eyelids. His elbow pulsed. He didn't even want to look at that massive scrape. His toes felt … cold and mushy, but at least they were quiet.

He snorted out of another nod. It seemed like he'd been copping a squat since forever, and not a peep out of the house the whole damned time. He'd get food and clothes for sure. If he was lucky, a clean towel and a bar of soap. He didn't need to scrub himself spotless, didn't need his goddamned 'Sunday Best.' He only needed to look good enough to turn himself in.

Last thing Lyle said to him was, 'Keep your mouth shut and let the lawyer do the talking.' Maybe the only thing he'd ever have to say about the whole fucking thing was 'Guilty.'

A townward motoring pricked him out of another drift. Firecracker pops spiked along the highway. The racket threatened a carload of Muellers. He held his breath. The gunned engine appalled him far away from any danger of falling asleep. The prick driver kept the pedal to the metal past the turnoff towards the house. Pud settled his forehead on his kneecaps. The clatter faded into the cricket chirps. The burden of his bony forehead irritated the scrapes beneath the grimy denim.

The next one might be them. One joint at a time, he crickled to his feet. He hobbled. The house had to be a million times worse than the way he left it. No way to clean it up good enough, his mother was gonna flip out no matter what.

He surveiled from the shed's edge. Everybody would find out they trashed the house. Everybody. Somebody would put one and one together. Somebody would wonder if the Muellers had anything to do with it, and the whole fucking thing would unravel. Fucking Los Bastardos would love to talk their shit to anybody who would listen, and everybody would just eat it up. Not even breaking silence, claiming it was an accident, would work then. The only way, the fucking only way, was to beat them to the punch. Confess. Everything.

Fuck.

Everything meant narking on Squint. Burying the body, the gun, and then all of it. No fucking way. So he had to convince them that he buried the body alone. He would probably have to sit in the witness box, just like on TV, while Tommy's mom wept and his dad stared burnholes into his son's murderer. His own mother would be too ashamed to show her face.

He glared. Of fucking course she would show up, probably wearing flipflops and all of it. She'd wanna make sure everybody knew she was disowning him, and she'd wanna make sure he knew that she'd been right to want to be rid of him all along. Took almost nothing to convice her to let him stay behind for their 'vacation.'

His hectic shrug crooked his neck. No. A dude like Tommy wouldn't have bothered if she was right. Tommy owned up to it and ate shit that he didn't have to eat. Tommy got out of that ring …

Toothy grins heehawed and rosied around him. He tottered. He clutched the shed's open corner. He straddled the framepost. *He caught him off guard …* His weight rolled onto his toes. Pain blasted it all away. He rocked onto his heels. The nuclear agony faded. Night smeared back into focus … *because he kept going.*

He growled towards the house. He banged his foot. His growl seethed between the cracks in his grinding grin. The house, its every fucking light blazing, riveted him. He steeled his fists. He exploded out of his limp.

Half the upstairs darkened. He hopped to a stop. He lowered his mangled foot onto the edge of the front lawn. On the other side of the house, the lesser bedrooms winked out, then the bathroom, shutting down the upstairs lights. Somebody making the rounds would head downstairs. He crouched within deeper shadow. He glimpsed a runtish figure in the kitchen before that room dimmed to the faint wattage of the sink light. In a rapid series, the frontside bulbs died, frustrating his attempts to get a good look at the Mueller, had to be a fucking Mueller.

He crept around the house. He edged up to the blue glow of first living-room window. The Mueller sank into the couch. The brighter TV flickers spotlighted his slackening expression. The stunted dude's sneakers dangled an inch or so above the floorboards. Pud expected to see about a hundred Muellers crashed out all over the house, not just the one sitter. He glanced behind himself. Only a few cars. Upstairs, there could be dozens sleeping or doing whatever.

His move towards the garage ignited his mangled foot. *Fuck this.* He stormed the front door. He ripped his favorite sickle out the backrest of the davenport. The fuckers had gone psycho, slashing upholstery all over the fucking room. His heels crunched glass. He kicked a beer can. The hollow aluminum rattled right at the Mueller, who'd circled behind the coffee table.

Kung Fu chops thwacked from the late late movie. Pud, with the length of the coffee table between them, watched the flickering of the TV strobe off the tiny dude's bald spot. Pud reeled against the arm of the couch.

The Mueller scurried around the other side of the table. Pud had to make sure and run the little fucker off. He pushed himself up off the couch. Across the debris of the dining room, a bigger Mueller stood in front of the little one. The bigger one backed into the runt.

Behind them, the windowpane reflected a psycho slasher, a slouched, devil-haired, hook-handed nightmare. Pud sneered. He faked a Frankenstein stomp. The Muellers bolted for the door, which swung in at them. The big one reared. The runt headbutted into the bigger one.

A dude blocked the threshold. He flipped his bangs out of his eyes, threw his head back, and cut loose a howl. His jean vest shrouded the prison-tat scrawl staining his bony chest. His Jovi-mane put the monkish bowlcuts of the other two to shame. The rocker gawked at Pud. "Holy shit," he said.

A shaggy blur bowled aside the dude's knees. Pud flinched. He swung at the thing. The flat of the sickle swatted the freak, who plowed through trash and thumped into the wall. Glass crackled. A bare heel banged against the floorboard. The freak's moan sounded female. Her hand-me-down jean shorts, two sizes too small, and her tube top identified her as a human. A girl. A small girl with really fucking long hair.

"Jesus Christ man," the rocker said. "You tried to kill her too."

Pud faced the other Muellers. "She came right at me!" His own whiny tone prickled him. This wasn't his fault. Hell, none of this shit was his fault. "I'm turning myself in!"

"You can't," the runt said. "You can't tell!"

"Yeah," the rocker said. "Nobody'll believe you anyhow."

Pud glowered. *Fucking idiots.* "No! I'm turning myself in for murder."

The Mueller girl untangled her thin limbs and scooted herself around onto her ass. From behind strings of dirty blond hair, black eyes glittered. She grunted. "They'll get you to tell," she said.

She flew at him. He raised his forearms. Her nails hooked the into the scrape on his elbow. He howled. The sickle clunked against the floor. He tore away from her. Around the wound, the skin shifted under his palm. He staggered.

She scooped up the sickle. Her eyes crossed while she studied the tip, while she skimmed a bloody fingertip along the curve of the blade. Her admiration crueled towards Pud.

She wouldn't dare.

She slashed. He contorted. The sickle grazed the tee-shirt billow over his stomach. She backslashed. The outer edge of the blade thudded against the underside of his chin. His neck whiplashed. He shuttled away from her, backing into the living room. He recoiled from another slash. The coffee table cut him off behind the knees. He keeled over. His ass bammed against damp carpet. His shoulderblades wedged against the base of the couch.

She pounced onto the table between his calves. He drew his legs back and tried to thrust the table over, but his heels slipped off the edge. The wobble made her cackle. He saw red. He jammed his back against the couch. He jackknifed his legs into the table. She yiked. The table skudded out from under her. She faceplanted.

Pud focused his eyes. He felt himself moving, revolving, trying to get the fuck up, but he seemed to revolve one grain at a time. She rose to all fours. She dog-shook her mess of hair. Her hand crawled towards the handle of the sickle.

"Shit," the rocker said. "Let's get him before he accidentally kills her."

Pud burped out, "I told Lyle!"

The Muellers halted.

Pud swallowed, found his voice, and said, "I told him I killed Tommy!"

The big Mueller shrugged at the others. He started towards Pud. The other two backed him up.

Pud squirmed backwards. "He went to get the cops," he said. He licked his lips. "They're coming straight here to pick me up."

"Shit," the runt said.

The rocker backhanded the big Mueller on the shoulder and said, "We gotta get out of here." He scooped up the girl up by the waist. She put up a weak fight. He cuffed her upside the head. She yowled, but she settled down.

Pud waited until he heard their engine fire up before he went to the windows. He watched the one working taillight vanish down the lane. They might stay away for good. Or they might decide to try to beat the cops back here, and those motherfuckers weren't coming.

Chapter Eighteen

"I see you," Pud said, "you motherfuckers. Bet you wish you could see me."

He couldn't really see them. But since he got his shit together, he'd watched the station wagon roll from the hill to the highway, pull a U-ey, and tool up the hill again, once with headlights on, this last pass lights out all the way around. Instead of disappearing into the hills, the wagon had looped into the grove half way up the rise. He knew exactly which tree hid the parked Muellers.

He knew they couldn't see him. Maybe on the porchlight side, but not up here against the empty tank. He'd killed sixers up here on the catwalk. He'd bogarted bowls while ducking moochers. At every goddamned one of his mother's 'socials' he'd swiped wine and nursed the jug from up on high, and even though the very last bitty sometimes didn't leave until after dinnertime the next fucking day, they'd never caught him, not once. Might look dumb, might look like he'd treed himself on the old grain tower, but there was no way they were gonna sneak up on him now. The rungs bolted onto the stanchion allowed one climber at a time, and if they tried it … he hefted the sickle.

Another gust disturbed the catwalk. Another spitting of raindrops strafed across the bridge of his nose. His shivers aggravated his busted toes. He had to keep all his weight on his heels. He couldn't stretch out his elbow or he'd rip that giant scab. He could walk and climb, but he didn't think he could run if he had to. He couldn't work up the nerve to take off his shoe and sock.

He whispered, "Forget about flipflops." He snorted. He would never have to hear them say that he thought he was too good for flipflops. Probably have to wear them in prison, in the showers, *gross*, just like in the lockerroom showers.

He scratched himself. "Goddamn them." Didn't matter. They only had to say one thing and whatever he said wouldn't matter at all.

Run away. Just run away. He should've done it a long time ago. They all wanted him gone anyways.

He hugged himself through another chilly gust. There was nowhere to run. He hated camping. He didn't think he could hack living like the riverbillies. Didn't matter anyways, even if he traced the river past the last squat in the hills, those freakass squirrels would no doubt sniff him out, probably Squint himself would lead the fucking pack.

He pulled his good knee up inside his arms. None of this was his fault. None of it. First Squint wanted to die, then he wanted to live so he could get his brains fucked out. He was the pervert. Pud squirmed to get comfortable on the metal gridding under his ass. Wasn't his fault. Nobody could've helped it.

He jerked his chin off his chest and glared at the starless sky. He wouldn't be like them. None of them had ever come close to doing what Tommy tried to do. Instead, they probably laughed about it all the fucking time.

He hurried his stare toward the grove. He'd lost their exact hideaway. By now they could've slipped out of the wagon, freaked themselves into squirrels, and started sneaking his way. Something big lurched out of the tree cover. Pud sniffed. The thing trundled over the shallow ditch, only resolving into the shape of the wagon against the pale road. Of course it was the wagon. None of the freaks he'd seen were anywhere near that big.

The station wagon traveled at little more than an idle as it coasted down the hill and turned onto the lane. The dimmest reaches of the porchlight's glow revealed the wagon's paneling. The woodish strips gleamed like new in the dark.

The wagon passed underneath the grain tower. Pud peered into the rear passenger window. The glass reflected a warped image of the house. Smudges clouded the glass. Underneath the reflection, he spotted a forked beard, or maybe the furry muzzle of one of those freaks.

The wagon's engine died before the vehicle rolled to a dead stop. *Closer to the house.* His spot was good. Better than good. *Perfect.* Anyways, they would've sent more if they meant to hurt him. They had to know there was nothing they could do now that he'd told Lyle the whole story. They would search the place and think he was long gone.

Car doors opened, none shut. Pud counted six by the way their footsteps fanned out. For sure one was scuffling away from the house, towards the grain tower.

"We …"

The callout startled Pud.

"… know you're around. I can smell ya. I can smell that you're close enough to hear me."

Fuck. Should've thought of that. But the dude sounded like he was talking to the house. And he didn't sound mad, he sounded almost wimpy. Still that lone Mueller's feet sifted gravel in the dirt lane, slacking towards the tower.

The wimpy one, still visiting with the house, said, "Looks like the pigs are little bit late."

The ranging Mueller whisked through the grass below the other side of the catwalk. Pud inhaled. No weresquirrel funk, but the river rot almost choked him.

"We don't wanna hurt you," Wimpy said. "We just wanna talk."

Pud aimed for absolute stillness.

"Don't wanna come out, huh? That's okay. We just wanted to remind you to keep your fucking mouth shut. You know exactly what I mean."

A dull ping vibrated from below. Pud pictured a biker-gloved palm slapping down on a rung. Maybe testing the bolts, maybe just fucking around. The Mueller couldn't like the looks of the uneven file of halfpipes. *Long way down motherfucker.*

"Nobody would believe you anyways," Wimpy said. "Just think you're crazy. But say they did believe you. You blow us up, we'll kill everybody you care about. Everybody."

Pud's left arm spasmed.

"Your mama," Wimpy said. "Your brothers and sisters. All your kin, maybe even track down your daddy."

Go right ahead.

"All you got to do is keep your fucking mouth shut, and we're quits. Swear on it, on a stack of Bibles ten feet tall."

Pud braced himself for the catch.

"We ain't liars … kinda looks like you are, though. If you were bullshitting about the cops coming to fetch you, then maybe you're bullshitting about all of it."

Pud strained to hear. He could've swore he heard a boot heel thunk against metal. Maybe they didn't even need the rungs. Just do their freak thing and scuttle up …

"Plan B is just to kill your ass. Got a bunch of dudes lining up for that honor."

Pud didn't want to think about how many Muellers might be roughing it along the river.

"But why would you even come back here, is what I can't figure out. Everybody says you ain't stupid. Maybe you confessed to that old motherfucker cop. I don't know. Makes my head hurt thinking about it."

Just go away then.

"By the way, Squint told us everything. Broke down bawling and everything. We know you was only trying to be a good bud, and shit just got out of hand."

He sounded as sick and tired as Pud about all this fucking shit. *Please, just go away then.*

"All he wants is to chase after that fat piece of ass. And he's gonna go over for good soon, so he's got nothing to lose by fucking you in the ass."

Below, a steeltoe tapped metal.

"We'll always be watching you. We got gobs of kin behind bars, we can get to you anytime we want. So keep your fucking mouth shut."

You keep your mouths shut, motherfuckers.

He lost the retreat of the Mueller below him when a motor started up, and then another, and another. *Good.* They were taking their piece of shit cars with them. He watched the convoy head down the lane, then disappear over the hill. They had better keep their mouths shut, because he figured a ton of whackjobs would believe him enough to come hunting for freako squirrels.

Chapter Nineteen

Pud tossed the sickle. The tool whiffled the tall grass and thudded near the bottom of the ditch. He'd sighted Lyle's mailbox. No mistaking that cartoony signboard of a sooped-up tractor pulling a wheely. So far only his soles's patter disturbed the highway. Better that Lyle didn't see him come dragging his foot and brandishing a weapon first thing in the morning.

He gritted his teeth and kept his bad toes up off the concrete, even though he'd just about walked the rubber off the back of his heel, even though he was murdering the last good part of his foot. Maybe Lyle would lend him a pair of shoes. Maybe Lyle would take a look at his foot. Pud swore to never walk anywhere again unless he absolutely had to. Maybe he could talk Lyle into calling an ambulance.

Just a little farther.

Close enough now to catch the snorks and herks of Lyle's hogs. The cresting sun warmed Pud's cheeks, but he'd yet to sweat his only polo shirt, a loaner from he didn't know who for his junior yearbook photo. He clucked his tongue. He'd blown off school that day and spent the five bucks. Never have to worry about scrounging up beer money again.

Dewdrops twinkled against the green of Lyle's lawn. The driveway ran straight upside the house to a fancy cement barbecue pit. Pud remembered when Lyle demolished his garage to put up the basketball court on the other side of the pit. He'd heard all about the Barbecue League.

Lyle stepped out of the house's side door. His pressed Levi's made Pud's jeans seem a little less shitty, for sure good enough for turning himself in. Lyle's dentures flashed against his flush. "Olds is in the barn," he said. "Everybody's waiting on us."

Pud limped behind Lyle. He hustled to match older man's bouncy pace. Pud ignored the blips pulsing from his mangled toes. He planned to set his seat in the Olds as far back as it would go.

Lyle fussed with the barn's access door, swinging open the bottom section. He gestured at the shut top section and said, "You got to duck inside." Lyle managed an awkward hunch. He crabbed through the opening. Hopeful whines arose among the hogs' snuffles. Pud strained to bend his blown legs low enough to dip under the jammed half of the door. Lyle said, "I already slopped you dang hogs, so shut up."

Once Pud stepped inside, Lyle worked on resetting the lower door. He muttered cusses aimed at the barn's back wall, at his hogs stamping around in the pen out back. Pud waited for his eyes to adjust. Pigshit hampered the porkers' hooves, suckling like bare feet squishing the required antiseptic mat on the way into the locker room showers. Bright blurts bent into orbit around his head.

"*Shit!*"

Pud started. Slatted rays teemed with dustmites at the other end of the barn. A greyish tarp covered the Olds. Pud stepped out from under the hay mow. A plank wall divided the barn in half, from one end almost to the other. Pud nodded. So that's why Lyle didn't need a garage. He just parked where a tractor was supposed to go.

Hands snatched Pud back into darkness. They held him down. They ducktaped his mouth, they hogtied his hands behind his back and left him sputtering on his belly in the moldy straw.

"That'd be a 4H record."

Pud stilled. *Matt.* That meant they were all here. Except for fucking Squint. Pud settled his bad foot into the least painful spot he could find.

"Where's the other one?" Lyle said.

"Didn't tell him," Kevin said. "Nobody else knows."

"All right," Lyle said. "I served this turd up on a silver platter. The rest is up to you boys. Remember, everybody gets their hands dirty."

Lyle weaseled through the lower door and shut it behind himself. Nobody made a sound while the old man fucked with the latch.

"Okay," Kevin said. "Who's gonna go first?"

Sunlight flecked the redhead, who had to stoop to fit underneath the mow. The stringbean silhouette had to be Trent, the short thick one had to be Kyle.

"Draw straws?" Matt said.

The lone dry snap echoed.

"Once this starts," Kyle said, "it only ends one way."

The duct tape sealing Pud's mouth threatened to smother him.

Trent whispered, "You sure we'll get away with this?"

Pud's wet snorts drowned out their quarrel. He took the biggest hit of air he could and held it.

"... the hogs."

"Does that really work?"

"Yeah."

"Who says so?" *Kyle.*

"The old man says so," Kevin said. "He used to be cop. He knows."

A nailhead, jutting from the floorboard, jabbed into Pud's cheek. He wormed the nailhead's edge under the bottom strip of the duct tape gag. He shuddered against the urge to tear the tape off. He raised his head until the tape peeled away from his lower lip. He snuck a full breath.

"Fuck it," Kevin said. He stalked towards Pud. "I'll do it." He planted his boot against Pud's ribs and shoved Pud onto his side. Kevin's breath stank. "Don't you make a fucking sound," he said. He ripped the tape off of Pud's whole head. "Where's Tommy?"

"I have to take you," Pud said.

Kevin backhanded Pud across the mouth. Pud thought the whiplash hurt the worst. The knuckle divots on his face throbbed.

"Okay," Kevin said. "We knew he might try that. I'll hold him. You guys get his pants off."

Pud bucked but Kevin pinned him on his belly. Kevin's huge hand engulfed Pud's head and mashed his jawbone into the grimy wood. Kevin said, "Somebody bring those nutters over here."

Pud seized on exactly what Kevin meant. "Wait," he said. "Wait, it's way out there, past the Mueller's place, out on government land."

"Fucking river rats," Matt said. "You just love those Muellers, dontcha?"

Pud swallowed the 'We' he almost spoke, along with any notions of narking on Squint for his part in digging the grave. "He's buried deep, so the animals won't get to him."

"Motherfucker," Kevin said. "Where the fuck is he?"

"Frontage road, past the trestle," Pud said. There's those woods ... stream ..." he struggled to remember if there'd been two streams. He couldn't remember it like this, he had to see the hills and the woods to see the way.

"Fuck," Kyle said. Everybody else quieted. "We better let him show us just to make sure."

Chapter Twenty

Sunlight filtered through leaves, dappling the grave. Pud watched Matt's shape weasel out from behind Kevin's shadow. Pud braced himself for a punt in the ribs. The weasel's boot skimmed the peak of the pile at Pud's elbow. A few bits of dirt pelted his cheek. He kept his head tucked. The weasel's shadow darted back into the redhead's cinderblock-fisted outline. Pud stayed on his knees. At the edge of the trail, Trent threshed a patch of tall grass. His muttering twitched whenever he pivoted back on his tracks. Kyle waited, somewhere, back there. Lyle circled into sight now and then, patrolling the perimeter of the clearing. The fucking liar's holster rode high on his hip. His hand rested on the butt of his gun. His cop stare took turns crawling over everybody.

Prove it, the motherfuckers had the nerve to say, as if he'd led them out to the middle of Bumfuck Egypt to trick them. Like he had any chance of getting by them, even if the motherfuckers hadn't ruined his foot. He wriggled his fingers into the dry soil. Stony fragments scoured the pink skin under his nails. He scooped out another double handful and let the crumbles rain on top of the pile. A little deeper, not nearly so deep as he told the assholes, and he'd prove it all right.

He dug into the dirt. Something stiff jammed his middle finger. He shifted his hands so that he didn't unearth it. He deposited the scoop on the pile. He could pull it right out of the ground. Get the drop on Lyle and disarm the backstabbing motherfucker. Strand them here, take the Olds back to town and turn himself in. As long as the fuckers didn't call his bluff, he didn't need to worry if the gun would work.

Move, idiot! He leaned over to excavate around the gun. Agony shredded up his earlobe. Matt's shadow danced back into Kevin's. Pud winced through the worst throbs. He swallowed the urge to lunge for the gun.

A squat shadow swooped. Pud flinched. Kyle kneeled beside the grave, on the side of Pud's flicked ear. Kyle lowered his thick torso. He dug, a fuckuva lot faster.

Lyle yelled at Trent, "You help too."

Trent stopped muttering. He stomped over and bent down on the other side of Kyle. He mumbled, "Shit's fucking out." His skinny fingers swept at the dirt.

"He could get off on a technicality," Lyle said. "He gets a good lawyer, and with what's done so far …"

Trent whisked away some dirt. He grabbed a fistful and and held it. Kyle shrugged his shoulders.

Pud's glare traced the contour of the gun.

Looming behind Pud, Kevin said, "Don't gotta worry about technicalities."

Pud's eyes zeroed in on the dirt shrouding the trigger. He said, "You're doing this because you know you did wrong." Kevin's rage warmed Pud's backside. Pud narrowed his eyes. "Tommy knew it was wrong."

"You liked it," Kevin said.

No. "You made me."

"Say 'you liked it'," Kevin said.

"You creamed," Matt said.

Pud scrabbled for the gun. He shot Kevin. He shot Kyle. Matt tried to run. Pud shot him. Pud stood up and shot Matt again. Trent sprang to his feet. A shot cracked before Pud could squeeze the trigger. Trent went down. Lyle, from the edge of the clearing, aimed at Pud, two-handed, crouching cop-style. Pud squeezed the trigger. His gun clicked. Lyle's shot whizzed past his shoulder.

Pain scorched up from Pud's bad foot, buckling Pud's first step towards cover. He tumbled across the grave. He rose to his hands and one good foot and ran like a three-legged dog. Lyle blasted away. Pud smashed into the brush. A few trees in he pawed up a trunk and onto his good foot. Clutching handholds among the branches, he bashed a one-legged slalom up the hill.

The woods thinned to a stony patch at the crest. He lurched across the gap. The crackle of crushed twigs exposed Lyle's position, way too fucking close to the bald hilltop. Pud plunged into the downhill thicket. He bulled through the tangles clogging the valley. The steep rise of the next hill sapped his arms and good leg. He paused at the ridgeline and caught his breath. Lyle had given up the coppish stealth, but he had lost ground, his crunching barely past the asscrack of the valley.

Pud hurried to the trees across the way. He slung himself from trunk to trunk down the slope. At the bottom a creekbed split the woods. Yellowish foam scummed the muddy seepage. A dirt path, a tree or two deep, traced the winding creekbank. He chose the darker turn. He hushed through the overgrowth. Smashes riffled about halfway back up the hill. Pud figured the old man had fallen flat on his ass.

The trail jagged into the woods. The thickening shade chilled Pud. The trail spread to a campsite. Kitchen chairs surrounded a circle of stones. Yellow padding showed through the holes in the shabby backs of all five chairs. A kink in the metal leg of one chair left its seat tilted toward the charred sticks of kindling. The blackened sticks made a perfect X that reached the edges of the stone circle. Pud gave wide berth to the chairs. The path narrowed. Itchweed crowded the dirt slash back towards the creekbank.

The trail forked. One path led to a plank that sagged across the creekbanks. The woods on the other side looked just as crammed as on this side. He peered at the plank. He stuck to this bank.

Weed clusters tapered the trail. Trunks closed in, forcing Pud sideways. The trail petered out into a thatch of brambles. Seed pods spiked his shirt and jeans. He shouldered into the brittle stalks and vines. A rusted barbwire fence halted him. He squeezed along the fence to the creek bank. The fence draped right over the water and disappeared into the woods on the other side. The woods swallowed the fenceline on this side. No telling where it ended, either way.

Fuck the noise, fuck his foot, he had to beat Lyle to that crossing. Pud bolted into the brambles. He smacked into Lyle's torso. The old man whoofed. Pud caromed into a tree. He hugged the bark. The old man wheezed. Lyle, on his back, clawed at his chest and neck. His grey face purpled. Pud limped over to the mashed stickyweed where Lyle had dropped his gun.

Pud shot Lyle still. He started back. To make sure of the rest.

Chapter Twenty-One

Pud used his good toe to goose the wooden swing's arc. His bad foot hovered over the dead dirt. He'd never do another jump bomb. Fuck it. He always hated the landings anyways.

Still, anybody would have to admit he'd done a pretty good job duct taping the fluffy white towel around his bad foot. Felt a lot better too, after showering it and then dumping all of Lyle's isopropyl on it. Pud palmed his right fist. Lyle's aluminum crutches leaned against the swingpole. An official Police gymbag rested on the circle of pole-anchoring cement. Lyle's house had all kinds of good stuff. The fucking faker sure as shit wouldn't need any of it anymore.

The swing's chains creaked. He couldn't detect another sound in the universe. He figured the cops would have surrounded him by now. Maybe they'd evacuated the town. Roadblocks and everything. But there hadn't been anything like that on the police scanner in the Olds. He shrugged. Maybe they'd known he was listening.

Past the far side of town, an engine muscled along the highway. The driver leadfooted it on the last open stretch. The engine drag-popped. The hotrodder shifted down to a cruise and cranked up the radio. Supertramp swelled. Pud grimaced. The white Trans Am swerved within a hair of the Olds' bumper and parked sideways to the curb, taking up three spots. Los Bastardos cut the music. Pud smiled. *Second best thing.*

Their untied laces flacked against their white leather hightops. They'd switched to stonewashed Levi's cutoffs for today instead of the usual basketball shorts, but they were sticking with those stupid red and white practice jerseys. Pud knew that their dark shades hid boozy eyes.

"Hey buddy," Greg said. "How's it hanging?"

Pud didn't bother to focus on Greg, who remained a black haired blob floating on his periphery. "I think I might have to go to the hospital."

Dean snickered.

Still, they make fun of me.

"So what the fuck are you doing here?" Dean said.

"Hoping to run into Squint," Pud said.

"You guys are the talk of the town," Dean said.

Pud glanced at Dean. Sunshine haloed the frizzy ends of his permed curls. "Oh yeah?" Pud said. "What are they saying?"

"They're saying one of you killed Tommy," Dean said.

"I did."

That did it. That finally shut their stupid faces up. Greg's crooked sunglasses made him look extra-special stupid.

"I knew he did it!" Dean gave Greg's shoulder a backhanded slap. "I told ya I told ya!"

"Bullshit," Greg said, while tagging Dean's bare shoulder. "He killed himself."

"Nuh-uh," Dean said.

Pud frowned. "I killed more than him," he said.

Greg pushed his sunglasses up his sweaty nose. "Yeah-huh," he said. "Everybody knows he was suicidal. Or Squint did it."

"The fuck," Dean said. "I keep telling you, that don't make no sense." Dean faced Pud. "Please tell him why you did it," he said. He swiveled and pointed at Dean. "Tell him it's because he named you 'Pud.'"

Pud's frown craggled. He raised his chin. In a way that was pretty close, but it sounded more, a lot more, like Dean didn't know shit …

"They call him 'Pud,'" Greg said, "because he swallowed Squint's pud."

Pud's spinal column jerked.

"Nah," Dean said. He pulled his fingerprint-smeared stainless steel flask out of his back pocket. "Tommy called him 'Pud' because he came buckets." He took a belt from the flask.

Pud inhaled enough air to ward the haze from his eyesight.

Dean passed the flask to Greg. "He jerked himself off," Dean said, "while he blew Squint."

Pud drew Lyle's gun out of the duffle bag and shot them. He rose out of the swing and shot them some more. Lyle's gun shot smooth. He shot them both dead. He picked up the flask and back-pocketed it. He stood over them. He whispered, "Fucking liars." The highway, fuck, the town, maintained its fucking Zen. "Where are the fucking cops?" He limped over to the crutches. Somebody had to have noticed all the shooting. He eyeballed the Trans Am.

Chapter Twenty-Two

Pud looked down on the FBI agents. Buzzcut, stared at the house while standing behind the open driver's side door. Curls walked the points around the Trans Am. From the catwalk, Pud couldn't tell if he was admiring the muscle car or searching for evidence.

Pud smiled. For all their fancy FBI skills, they were no better than all those moochers he'd ditched, or even his mother's stupid friends, didn't even glance at the grain tower. All he had to do was stay in the shadow. He patted Lyle's duffle bag. No way he could hit them from up here. Not that he wanted to. He just wanted to sit here in the shade.

He sighed. Tommy wouldn't do that. Anyways, he couldn't just pee off the other side. The agents couldn't be *that* stupid. "Hello!" he said. "I'm coming down!"

He didn't wait to see if they were gonna shoot him. Getting onto the rungs one-footed took up all his attention anyways. He lowered his good foot, chin-up style, one level at a time. They didn't say shit, all the way to the bottom of the tower, their tread kicking up dirt along the lane at barely more than an amble.

Pud grabbed Lyle's crutches. He wondered if these two sherlocks even noticed them leaning against the stanchion. He propped himself up and faced them.

"What were you doing up there?" Curls said.

"Where's your mother?" Buzzcut said. The fucker gave Pud a crinkly stinkeye, like maybe Pud had killed her too. Well fuck 'em. Starting right the fuck now, he was exercising his right to silence.

Curls twisted towards the Trans Am and said, "Nice car." His gray suit jacket opened to his hip, showing his strapped-in gun. Neither of them had handcuffs ready.

"Not talking," Buzzcut said. His starched white shirt collar bunched up his neck skin. "Doesn't matter. We know everything."

"We know all about your little grabass party," Curls said.

The younger agent had the nerve to wink at Pud. *Grabass? You don't know jackshit.*

"We know who was there," Buzzcut said. His blue necktie hung from a tightass knot. Pud wondered how the asshole could breathe. Buzzcut ran down the names, nailing each and every one. No more, no fucking less. " … we know who was watching, we know who had their pants down, we know who made who do what."

"We know why they call you 'Pud,'" Curls said. His blue eyes leered. "Hey," he said, his eyes softening, "so a little dribble came out. It happens."

Pud tilted back on the crutches until his back relaxed against the stanchion.

Buzzcut sniffed. "Okay, we'll do it the hard way." He about-faced and strolled towards their sedan. Curls followed his boss, muttering something about lawyers. Buzzcut called out, "He better have a damned good one."

What the fuck …

Chapter Twenty-Three

Fuck it.

Pud shoved the Trans Am's door open. He swiveled his good foot out onto the grass.

From within the house, a woman hollered, "Don't you make another move!" Her attitude chilled as she said, "We got guns too." Flies buzzed the screen door. Newspapers patched each busted-up window. Could be a million of them in there. Except that burnt popcorn and septic-tank stink would be way worse. He should have plowed right into their living room, but the shitty wooden porch looked tougher from a distance. He'd settled for locking up the brakes and skidding to a stop. The TA's fiberglass nose had nudged a railpost. The porch's roof had sagged, and now it looked like it might collapse under the weight of all those dead leaves at any second.

He slouched. The TA's door and frame gave his head decent cover. He rested his gun hand on the steering wheel. Trees from the woods gnarled right up to both sides of the house. Weeds crowded the gaps between trunks. A few junkers, all rust and Bondo, jammed up the roundabout in front of the house. The rut lane back to the dirt logging road curved out of sight into the woods. Shooters, or whatever the fuck, could have him completely surrounded for all he knew.

"There's still a way out of this for you," the woman called from inside, near the screen door. "Let me come out and talk to you."

The corner of Pud's mouth dimpled. *A way out.* They must've not heard about the … five, six … seven, *seven*, others he'd shot and killed. That made it eight, plus however many Muellers he was about take with him.

"We cleaned up your messes," she said. "The one in town wasn't easy." Darkness blotted most of the screen door's mesh. "Say you ain't gonna shoot."

"I'm not gonna shoot an unarmed woman." Pud licked his lips. "But if I see any bullshit …"

"No bullshit."

The screen door whinged open. Her first step made the porch creak. Pud glanced at the roof. *Dangling by a thread … ugggh.* Pud snorted the charred-popcorn musk out of his nostrils. He grimaced. He slitted his eyes.

One more step and she towered over the Trans Am's open door. Her brown frizz drooped to her shoulders. Her coke-bottle lenses shrunk her eyes to dots. "Your mother is on the way home," she said. The floral pattern of her long-sleeved green dress hid her shape, except for the bulges rolling down from somewhere around the top of her belly. "Somebody found her campsite, somebody got her a paper. I imagine she'll be home by tonight at the latest." She shifted from one foot to the other. Her massive hip, at a freakish height, strained fabric before her dress fell back into its formless hang. "Like I said, we cleaned up your messes, but that one in town," she produced a low whistle while shaking her shaggy frizz, "I don't know. All I know for sure is the cops never came."

"Cops …"

She nodded. "That's right, we got their bodies. We got all the bodies." She stared up the lane. "Squint told me everything." She worked her jowls. "How he was the one that got this whole mess started. I decided he'll take the blame." Her coke-bottle lenses trained on him. "Squint is gonna disappear for good pretty soon no matter what. If you're in jail, or dead, more likely, the way you're going, and Squint goes missing after, then folks are gonna keep snooping around like they been, but even more probably, probably more than one TV van this time too." She mouthbreathed a lungful. "This has got to stop. You come around to the old church after midnight and see for yourself. Squint's gonna call the cops and confess. When they come, he's gonna get himself shot dead. They'll find the bodies in the church, everything will look like he killed them and tried to fix the blame on you. And that will be the end of it."

She waggled her index finger at Pud. "First thing, now, you can't be seen in this car."

"I'll get rid of it." Pud fired up the engine before she could bitch about it. No way was he getting out of the Trans Am. He twisted between the seat and swerved the TA backwards up the lane as fast as he dared. *Just how stupid do you think I am?*

Chapter Twenty-Four

He got rid of the Trans Am. About ten minutes ago. As close as the woods behind the Old Church allowed. Well, he had to back up a little to get out of wedging the doors between two trees. A whiff of charcoaled popcorn kernels had reached him before he got himself up on Lyle's crutches. The smell had stewed during his meandering course through the trunks. They didn't say shit, though, the whole fucking time, while he felt his way through the darkness.

He crutched himself out of the woods. His good foot's landing crunched the dead leaves carpeting the church grounds. He centered himself on the crutches. He started his lap around the church. *Don't rush.*

An orange glow flickered through the cracks between shriveled planks. *Church.* Just another shitty barn. Didn't even have a steeplecross anymore. People said they used to have tent revivals on top of this hill, snake-handlers, jibber-jabberers, every fucking thing. Then some asshole built a tiny dump of a barn, out in the middle of the fucking woods, and called it a church. Now it was a place where kids smoked cigarettes and felt each other up, or big kids took little kids to scare them.

They would expect him to be scared shitless, they wouldn't expect him to charge straight in the doors. He spat on the leaves. He really didn't need to look around. How could they smell anything over their own funk?

Pud crunched through the leaves around a blackened bonfire pit. Whispers from whithin leaked out of the barn's plank siding. The churchy double doors didn't let out a speck of light. No cars in the front lot. The brambly side of the barn forced Pud to crush along close to the wall. He completed the circle and kept on to the footpath leading to the double doors.

He reached into the inside pocket of Lyle's flannel. He pulled out a pack of Lyle's smokes. Lyle had stashed away all kinds of good stuff. He racked a cigarette and struck a match. Motherfucker deserved to die. No telling what those assholes might've done to him. Those motherfuckers definitely deserved it. He lit the smoke. Los Bastardos ... well, their big mouths made it a thing, made it a worse thing, a thing that otherwise nobody might've known about.

He took a drag and exhaled. He liked their plan, with Squint taking the fall, but Pud thought he could make it better. He could confess what everybody craved to hear. Really give them their jollies. More lies to make the first one seem like truth. But that wasn't what Tommy would do. Pud took another drag. He shook his head. *Fuck Tommy.* Fucker was just as guilty as the rest of them.

His crutches jounced on the dead leaves. The charcoal lighter fluid cans, duct-taped upside down to the crutches' crossbars, you better believe the biggest cans Lyle could buy, the kind you had to squeeze to get a drizzle, rang hollow against the aluminum.

He touched the cigarette's coal to the matchbook, which was full minus the one. The matchbook torched. *This is gonna hurt like hell.* He sucked in a lungful. He dropped the fire on one of the lighter fluid cans. He rushed to the church doors while pulling the flask out of his back pocket. His foot screamed, but fuck it. He uncapped the flask. He doused the doors, splashing the last of the lighter fluid back towards the blazing cans.

He gimped as fast as he could to where the footpath met the dirt road. A heatwave staggered him. He retreated. He shielded his eyes. The church burned. The fire raged through the woods. *Fuck.*

A distant whoomph made him hunch. The forest fire had already swept over the gascan-loaded TA. Planks exploded over the roaring inferno. A burning figure blurred out of the smoldering haze and barreled into the cool side of the woods. Pud fumbled out his handgun. By the time he aimed, it wasn't worth pulling the trigger. *Probably fucking Squint.*

Chapter Twenty-Five

Pud jabbed the carcass with the barrel of his rifle. The freakass squirrel didn't respond. He stuck the barrel into the thing's bellyfat and rolled it onto its backside. Two shots in the head. *Not bad.* But the freak wasn't him. For one thing, this squirrel was a bitch. But the eyes weren't squinty enough, either. He'd discovered that some features persisted through the change.

He'd discovered a lot of things, in a relatively short span of time. And he suspected that the riverbillies knew things they weren't telling him.

He left the corpse. They took care of their own. Anyways, smart to skeddaddle before the pack showed up. Or the fucking cops, who still had their fucking questions. He would just keep ranging back this way now and again. He'd get that fucker sooner or later.

www.ingramcontent.com/pod-product-compliance
Lightning Source LLC
Chambersburg PA
CBHW070534130626
46555CB00003B/1407